Six Queens
&
A King

Six Queens
&
A King

CERYS BECKWITH

Cover art by Julia Reid

ISBN-10: 0692372067
ISBN-13: 978-0692372067

For women of the world who,
throughout time's many tribulations,
have held their heads high like queens.

A BRIEF NOTE

Kings and queens are fascinating subjects, locked into history by dates of reign, marriages, and alliances. By many means — both through barriers of time and a lack of information — we know very little about the personal lives of these royals. Of course, we understand the regulations they followed and lives they lived. A quick web search will show us what types of regal dresses they wore, how many servants they had, and the activities they engaged in from day to day. But a web search cannot spell out the thoughts of these unique characters.

Years ago, I was captivated by King Henry VIII and 16th century England. To begin with, the time period was intriguing. Furthermore, the fact that one king could have so many wives, each unique to the previous, captivated me. Yet, no factual book or documentary could reveal to me the emotions behind a noblewoman cast aside for a mistress, or the distress of a maiden waiting to die with a sword balanced above her neck. It seemed only right to, using the true facts of history, mold these queens into not just wives of a king, but into true characters of human power, pain, and perspective.

CONTENTS

In Catherine's Chambers   13

An Uncapped Vial   35

My Modest Maiden   57

Before Anne is Annulled   75

Flawed Pearls   89

For the King   107

Divorced

IN CATHERINE'S CHAMBERS

Catherine began to weep, her knees trembling. "This is certainly treason upon the English land, Majesty." Gripping the hand-carved wooden cross that dangled from a thin chain about her neck, she stepped forward and crossed onto the rug where Henry's throne rested. The king sat up straight and removed his feet from his footstool. The movement caused his jewels to shake and jangle together.

"Do not speak to me of treason," he said in return, voice rumbling. "I have been nothing but loyal to you and my people. Upon my brother's death, I did honor the tradition that I accept you as my own, as is the noble action. But now, our partnership does little for the state of England." Henry paused and looked up to Cromwell, his advisor.

"His Highness is not wrong, Lady Catherine," Cromwell added. His shoulders were pushed back, his chin held up as he looked down at Catherine from his high position. "The late king would be proud of your husband for the steps he now takes to improve the state of England through this split from the overbearing Pope."

Henry nodded and Catherine froze. She looked back and forth between the two lofty men, their sleek, bearded faces the depiction of arrogance. Releasing the cross from her tight grip, Catherine dropped her arms to her side. She took a step back and straightened her shoulders. "My Arthur would be in utter disgust of what you have confirmed today."

"Why, I have never been so – " Henry began, but was cut off by the clear voice of Catherine.

"This decision rejects all that he had stood for. It denies the people of a strict religion and casts aside those who have followed the glorious traditions of England all these past years. To say that Arthur would be proud – to even say that he would accept these changes, all for the sake of some silly maiden you wish to wed – is an offense to his name." Catherine tugged down the sleeves that had begun to ride up her arms. With a sweep of her hand, she brushed aside the loose wisps of hair that had fallen from her hat. She raised her chin high. Looking directly at the stone eyes of the king, Catherine said, "I see now how severely blind you are to these matters." She turned her gaze to Cromwell. "Both of you." Cromwell let out a murmur and moved to whisper to the king.

"The lack of respect with which you speak to your king is disgraceful," Henry retorted. "Yet, you were my brother's love, and I will show you mercy by removing you to another palace out of this land." Henry rose from his throne, the red backdrop behind him quivering as he did so. The king stepped forward and Catherine felt each of his footsteps through the wooden panels across the floor. He stopped in front of Catherine, standing with his hands at his waist while looking down at her. "A minute amount of respect is the least you ought to offer me."

From beyond where the pair stood, Cromwell chimed in. "An

apology ought to be in order, Lady Catherine."

The queen inhaled sharply. "The day on which you give respect to me and my people is the same day that you will receive any sort of apology from me." Henry's faced flushed red in anger, but Catherine held up a hand to silence him before he could respond. "It is clear that no progress will be made. If your decision is final, then I shall take my leave."

Henry looked past Catherine and nodded at the footman, who swung the door open and stood in silence by the exit. Without a word, Henry gestured to the door. Narrowing her eyes, Catherine pushed back her shoulders and turned to walk away. The black skirts of her regal dress skimmed against the ankles of the stubborn king.

***

With a vicious slam of her chamber doors, Queen Catherine of Aragon finally collapsed. She leaned back against the polished framework of her private room and clenched her eyes shut. They stung deeply.

"My Queen?" said a trembling voice from across the room.

Startled, Catherine stood up straight and pulled out a piece of spare cloth from beneath the strap of her dress. She dabbed at her watering eyes and mumbled, "Yes, it is I. Bess, is that you?"

Quick footsteps padded over the rough floor. Catherine felt the gentle hands of her personal attendant slip the crumpled cloth from her shaking hands. The young lady reached up and pulled loose the gable hood that clung to Catherine's hair. Taking up the handkerchief again, she wiped away the tears that traced streaks down Catherine's powdered face. "Oh, Bess," Catherine wept. "You cannot begin to comprehend what a day it has been." Bess stood stiff in shock, astounded to see her strong queen cry.

Gently, Bess touched the royal lady's arm and looked up to Catherine. "Let us refresh you, Your Majesty. Then, I will call for your ladies, and they shall come to comfort you in this time of distress."

"Goodness, no!" Catherine exclaimed. "Those spiteful faces are the last I wish to see at this moment. Please, Bess, let us take comfort in the privacy and silence of my chambers here for the afternoon."

Bess nodded her head, unable to retort against her queen's direct wishes. "Whatever pleases you most, My Lady. Mightn't we still refresh you?" Bess offered an arm, which Catherine daintily took.

In silence, Bess led her mistress to her dresser, pulling a cushioned stool out for Catherine. She sat down, intertwining her fingers. Bess smiled and curtsied to Catherine before she scurried off to the main chamber doors, her bare feet making little noise. She requested a small tub of washing water and waited for its arrival. A servant soon arrived. The sloshed water covering his front was a clear sign of his hurry. Thanking him, Bess wiped the wet side of the basin dry with her sleeve and turned back to her queen.

Eyes watering once again, Catherine stared at her reflection in the small round mirror on her wall. She reached up to run her thumb over the wood and traces of gold that laced the murky mirror.

"What a gorgeous headpiece you chose today, My Lady," Bess said. She placed the basin of water on the tabletop in front of Catherine. Attempting to distract the queen from her worries, Bess pulled the hat from her head and placed it to lie on its side. Its pentagon shape folded into itself, deflating.

"I suppose..." Catherine said. "Henry chose it for me, but I certainly prefer a more rounded, simple style myself."

"Of course, Your Majesty," Bess responded. "You have always been a lady known for her regard of simplicity and elegance."

Catherine offered no response or thanks to these comments, but continued gazing at herself gravely in the mirror. Bess touched Catherine's shoulder, then moved beside the water basin. She reached into the bowl, pulled out a soaking cloth, and wrung it out until it just barely dripped lukewarm droplets back into the basin. Keeping it bundled in her hands, Bess brought the damp material to her queen's face. She carefully rubbed off layers of powder from her creased skin. Catherine shivered and offered her hands to Bess. The young maid took her mistress's hands and placed them in the cooling water.

Catherine looked up, her eyes drooping. She raised a wet hand to trace her fingers over the dips of her face, her index finger following the lines that laced down her cheeks. "Bess..." Catherine said. "My days as queen have made me so old." Her voice split with a quiver.

"Do not say that, My Lady." Bess once again placed Catherine's hand in the basin. "You are just as exquisite as when you were first betrothed to your dear King Henry."

"Today it was made clear that he does not believe that is true," Catherine bit back, pulling her hands from Bess's and running them over her face. Water splashed from the basin. Bess fell to her knees to dab up the liquid with a dry cloth. Meanwhile, Catherine scrubbed at her face, leaving her round cheeks red, and the grey under her eyes exposed. With a sigh, Catherine rested her elbows on her dresser and let her head drop into her cupped hands.

Bess rose from the floor. "My Lady, your appearance is still lovely." Bess grabbed a fine comb from the dresser and retreated behind Catherine. Releasing her tangled hair from its knot, Bess said, "Look at your deep golden hair. Many women, royal and common, only dream of having hair as radiant as yours." Bess reached forward to lift Catherine's chin, forcing her to face the mirror once again. "Take a look at your eyes, as well, Your Majesty," the maid said, tugging the comb through the snarls of

Catherine's hair. "They are so deep a blue, not unlike the sky one sees just beyond the rocking ships once the sun has set. You are blessed with such beauty." Bess hesitated before adding, "And Princess Mary, daughter of His Majesty and yourself, shares in your appearance. The king is delighted in what a daughter you pair have produced. He could not be happier with the life you do share."

"Bess, do not so blatantly lie to me," Catherine countered. "It is common knowledge around the castle that there are but days remaining before my time here as queen is ended." Catherine's voice cracked once again, and a tear escaped her eyes.

Bess stared. With her thumb, she wiped the damp streak from Catherine's face. "My Queen, perhaps you exaggerate so. I hear – "

"Do not bother," Catherine interrupted. "During my meeting with the king today, it was made apparent to me that little hope remains of my life here at Hampton Court. Anne Boleyn, Henry's third mistress during our marriage, continues to seek control of the throne. She holds the king's heart as I once held Arthur's, and no logic can seem to penetrate such strong emotions."

Astounded, Bess said, "Why, perhaps... But this Boleyn woman has no more hope of taking your crown than did Bessie Blount or Mary Boleyn. Each has met her downfall in greed."

"Yes, but this Boleyn has sway and power far beyond that of those previous women. I... you see..." Catherine's words faded in and out as her hands came together to rest upon her stomach. Her voice a whisper, she said, "They do now say that Anne Boleyn is with child."

Bess's eyes widened. "Then she most surely will not be taken into the royal court! A tainted woman such as – "

Catherine burst out into a fit of distraught laughter. Bess shrank back into herself, watching her queen bend over, veiny hands gripping the edge of her dresser to keep from falling to the floor.

Bess turned from Catherine, tucking away the washcloth and combs. "Oh, Bess," Catherine coughed out between laughs. "I so do wish I had your youth, your naiveté, still to this day." Catherine turned on her stool to face Bess directly. "Don't you see, my dear? The child that Anne begins to nurture is fathered by my husband, the king."

Bess froze.

Catherine nodded solemnly.

"It..." Bess croaked out. "It is gossip, I am sure, My Lady."

"Hardly," Catherine retorted, returning to her original position by the mirror. "The king has already made the decision to split from Rome and promote himself as head of our great Catholic Church for this woman and her conceived child." Catherine's hands balled into tight fists as she spoke. "The scandal is horrific."

Bess stood in shock. "Queen Catherine, I... This is terrible news."

"Truly so," Catherine responded. Her chest rose and fell unsteadily as she attempted to regain her composure. "The affair is so poorly concealed, as well. Today, before things went so wrong at court with Henry, a select few of my ladies and I were waiting by the gates for a carriage to take us into town for some circulating. George, the head stable hand you always seem to have a open ear for – "

Bess blushed and opened her mouth to retort, but words seemed to fail her. Her cheeks glowed even redder at her mistress's chuckle.

"Oh yes, Bess. I may be old now, but I still recognize those looks of admiration. How I had longed to receive such a glance from Henry upon our engagement..." Catherine stared off into the mirror, almost as if searching for something beyond the placid image laid out in front of her. Her cheeks still glistened with drying tears. "I apologize, dear, I seem to have lost my point."

Bess cleared her throat. "Yes, hmm, you were discussing something about George and a carriage to town, My Lady...?"

Catherine's face fell once again. "Of course. George approached our small cluster and asked if I would be joining the king for his afternoon ride. Naturally, I was confused. The king takes his rides in the early morning, and very rarely requests that I, let alone my ladies, join him. He deems me to be a poor rider. So I responded that I would not be accompanying him, as I had time scheduled in the town for the upcoming hours. A perfect gentleman, George nodded his head and proceeded to ask whether that meant he should stow away the second horse." Catherine smiled pitifully. "*What second horse?* I asked. George frowned and said, *why, it was requested of me that I prepare two horses for His Majesty, as a good friend would escort him.*" Catherine shook her head. "The king has so few close friends, and none of them are men from the palace."

"My Lady," Bess chimed in. "There are still many assumptions being made here."

"Why, you did not let me finish," Catherine said, a sharp sting tipping on the edge of her words. "My suspicions arose, and I requested that George prepare both horses and attend to *every need* of the king's *good friend*. I offered him compensation if he would only return to me after their leaving and describe to me the physical appearance of the king's companion."

"So I did wait." Catherine let out an unsteady breath. Recovering her poise, she continued, "I cancelled the carriage. My ladies and I waited in the garden by the court's entrance. George returned, and he described to me an intriguing woman. *Her hair was a dark brown, though under the trees it appeared almost black,* he told me. *Her skin was darker than that of any woman I have ever witnessed walk these grounds, though her features seemed just slightly contorted. Not necessarily a pretty thing. Though she wore a thick red dress that did sweep over her mare's hindquarters in a rather elegant fashion.* The truth was clear. Henry had taken to the woods with none other than one of my own ladies in waiting, Anne Boleyn." Catherine choked on the name. "I sent George away so I might discuss matters with my ladies alone. As we sat in the gardens exchanging judgments, the king and his company went striding past. My husband led the group, a wilting rose tucked into his crooked jacket, his chest held high and a typical smug smile on his face. I moved to confront him, and requested yet another counsel. Later in the throne room with his advisor, my fears were finally confirmed." Catherine's face was wet again. "After all these years of quarrelling over the matter, the king has declared an official split, from both myself and glorious Rome." Catherine cried out and hid her face.

"Oh, My Lady," Bess murmured, her eyes welling up with sympathetic tears. "There must be something to be done."

Catherine looked up and roughly wiped beneath her eyes. "There is not. I cannot sway a decision that has already been made. My heart aches that the church must be divided from our great kingdom for such lustful and illegitimate reasons. But King Henry must have his male heir, and he deems it necessary to use a method so vile as a separation of our marriage to achieve such means." A sigh escaped Catherine's lips. "There is no hope that I might offer him such a son, now. I have aged so. A forty-two year old woman such as myself cannot hope to bear a child that will last through the sicknesses and pains of the years. Numerous times I have attempted to give life to a child, but the only who has lived is my precious Mary. The others suffered their early fates either in the womb or shortly thereafter..." Catherine wiped away the tears that were slipping down her face.

"Why, Your Majesty, I am terribly sorry."

"You owe me no apology, Bess," Catherine said. "Many men and women of this castle owe me their repentance, but you are not among them. In your few years of service, you have been nothing but a friend and civil confider to me."

Bess blushed and ducked into a curtsy. "Thank you, My Queen."

Catherine nodded. "Speaking of our relationship during this time together, there is something that you must be informed of before I do leave these chambers evermore."

"Yes, My Lady?" Bess prodded.

"Promise me you will not think me an insane woman," Catherine said, her eyebrows scrunched together with worry. She gestured to a stool beside her, and Bess sat.

"The thought would never cross my mind, My Lady."

Catherine's shoulders fell and she smiled weakly at Bess. "Now," Catherine began. She leaned back against her dresser and folded her hands across her lap. "I must admit to you that for these few months past, I have been gathering a story from truths that have spread around this castle, and I now believe I understand the sources of my misfortunes."

Raising her eyebrows, Bess looked to Catherine. "Yes… and what is it that you have discovered, My Queen?"

"Anne, the king's most recent mistress…" Catherine paused and for a moment, a hint of doubt passed across her face. With a blink of her eyes, it vanished. In a whisper, she continued. "She is a witch."

Bess couldn't contain the laugh that shot through her chest. "That is quite an accusation to make, Your Majesty!" she giggled. "An affair with a witch?"

The stern, offended look that had been forming on Catherine's expression dropped from her face. "When you put it in such blunt terms, I suppose it does sound preposterous," she said. "Nevertheless, when I present my evidence, you shan't find the theory quite so outlandish," she insisted.

Bess nodded, gesturing for Catherine to continue.

"When I first heard of Anne's entrance into my courts, I was rather flustered. Her sister, Mary, had relations with my husband previously, and it seemed odd that another of the family should become one of my ladies in waiting. In my spare time, I set out to learn more about the maid, and there was much that I discovered." Catherine noticed her shoulders had stiffened, and allowed them to relax with a slow, calculated exhale. "See, Anne was originally of the court of Margaret, an elegant Archduchess whom I have never had the fortune to meet. She then moved to the household of Mary, my lord's sister, the wife of King Louis XII. Even with the death of the French king, she remained a lady in the French house. She attended to Claude, the next queen, for nearly seven years, and gained much favor with the French people. Her position – "

"M-might I interrupt briefly, My Lady?" Bess said. "You say that your history overlaps, yet I see no cross."

"I am providing background for the matters at hand," Catherine retorted, waving a hand at Bess's comment. "You must understand her relation to the French line, else you cannot hope to grasp her relation to myself." Catherine paused to give Bess a chance to respond, but the girl remained silent. "As I was saying," she chided in annoyance, her fingers shaking against the fabric of her dress. "Her position put her in a place of reasonable sway amongst those royals close to her. This makes me believe that she may have been present at the Field of Cloth of Gold. Here, my Henry did meet Francis I, the French king. These things I know to be fact," Catherine said, leaning forward. "I gathered this information from my remaining friends back at my home in Spain, along with a variety of members of this court."

"The remainder is assumption, Your Majesty?" Bess questioned.

Catherine fidgeted. "Assumption based on solid observation."

She looked up to Bess once again. "Many a lady have aspired to be the wife of the great King Henry," Catherine continued. "One of the many women who fell for him might well have been Lady Anne Boleyn." Catherine sniffled and a soft sob escaped her throat at the mere idea she was proposing. "He was a man very suiting to her kind. A few occasions before, Anne attempted to raise herself in status. A marriage between the heir of Ormonde and herself once fell through. She also attempted to form an affair with both Henry Percy, a fairly wealthy heir, and the poet Thomas Wyatt."

Bess glanced up. "Why, Sir Wyatt has been married many a year, My Lady!" exclaimed Bess.

"From what you have thus learned of this woman, do you truly take this as a surprise?" Catherine rebuked.

Bess shook her head.

"Quite. Now, I have digressed from the matter at hand... I suspect that Anne, as she had done many a time before with other men, had attempted to woe my Henry upon meeting him. With his wealth, power, and honor, there is no doubting the possibility that Anne could have fallen for Henry, as many who came into meeting with the man did." Catherine paused. "I surely did at first."

Waiting just a moment, Bess reached over and placed her hand atop Catherine's and gave it a reassuring squeeze. Catherine took a breath and used her free hand to wipe away the tears that were beginning to roll down her face. "Being that so many passionate women hold jealousy in their hearts, I do not doubt that this *witch* holds a deep grudge against my life and well-being," Catherine concluded, spitting out the accusation.

Bess took both of Catherine's hands in hers. "My Lady?" she said timidly. "Though your story may hold some truth, it rests on a great deal of your heart and emotion. It worries me that you are blinded by your anger."

Catherine blinked and met Bess's eyes with an angry gaze. "Do you not believe me?"

"I did not make such a claim, Queen Catherine!" Bess rushed to respond. "It simply felt wise to point out that there are remaining incongruences in your tale."

"Of course there are," Catherine retorted. "But I have evidence yet. I lost four sons, one in womb and three just after I did give them life. By first thought, I assumed such losses to be due to my own body's natural flaws. Yet, seventeen years ago I did birth a beautiful young lady, my darling Mary. She has thrived, as any other child might. Yet, despite such a success, I still did fail to bear another healthy child. Even when my pregnancies felt beyond blessed, their terms were brief and sorrowful. Doctors did not understand why such things troubled me." Catherine's voice broke, her hand tightening around Bess's. "Now I do see a new truth. Anne has bewitched my womb to prevent me from bearing a male heir for Henry."

Bess sat and considered what Catherine had laid out before her. "Yes..." she mumbled, releasing Catherine's hands. She looked up and met Catherine's searching gaze, tilting her head. "Majesty, I do see the likelihood that unnatural spirits tampered with your capabilities as a birth mother. But there are many a witch that roam through England. How can you be so sure it is Anne who harms you?"

"I do try ever so hard to avoid making enemies. Even when my actions have accidentally provoked anger, I have made sure to seek out the victim and make amends. For days, I have searched for some other foe, some poor man or woman whom I may have offended and thereby received this punishment. Anne is the only one who holds the power and reason for these crimes." Catherine's eyes narrowed. "Understand that I do not make these accusations lightly, Bess. It is only after weeks of development that I cautiously come to these conclusions."

"Of course," Bess scrambled to reply. "My Lady, though you feel your age has made you weak, it has only made you wise. I do not doubt your belief in the matter. I do, however, question why you have invited me to share in this knowledge you have attained."

"When I am so unfairly thrown from this castle which has made itself my home these past years, a great deal will change," Catherine said. She released the tautness from her hands, blood flowing back to her whitened knuckles. "The sanctity of marriage will be abandoned once I have been dismissed, and a social upheaval will occur. Divorce will taint the purity of the royals. I tell you these things so you shall not be deceived as so many others have. You must keep close eye on Anne and her behaviors around the king. Your duties over these chambers will transfer to her, so I doubt this task will be difficult. I would not ask of you such a chore did I not think it safe."

Catherine stopped and rose from her seat. She straightened her skirts and offered an arm to Bess. "I understand, My Queen," Bess replied, taking Catherine's arm and following her on wobbling legs over to a window facing the courts of the palace.

Catherine glanced down to the courtyard. "I must ask of you one other selfish deed," Catherine said, eyes following some movement down across the grass below. Bess leaned forward and, following Catherine's line of sight, saw a teenage girl, fitted in a dark blue dress, strolling through the gardens. "Please watch over my Mary," Catherine said. She gestured to the girl. "She is no longer a child, but I still fear what her life will hold once I have left."

"My Queen, I seem not to understand your implications... Will Princess Mary not accompany you when you leave?"

"No," Catherine responded, looking away from her daughter. "Though she is a girl, she still remains the sole heir to the king's throne. He would never allow her outside of these walls to stay with me. This much I know for certain." Catherine turned from the window, dropping her arm from Bess's and wandering back into the room. Bess turned to watch the older woman drift about the room, fingers fumbling across the tops of chairs and dressers that she had known so well for over twenty-four years.

Bess approached Catherine and placed a hand on her shoulder. "My Lady, no harm shall come to any child of yours while this court still employs me," she said. "Neither man nor nature nor spirit will touch the daughter of one who has become so dear to me."

Silence dropped over the two women as Catherine turned to face Bess. She reached forward and embraced the young maid, feeling her lively heartbeat against her chest. "I cannot thank you enough," she said, pulling back and placing her hands on Bess's shoulders. Catherine smiled and lifted a hand to wipe away the tears that were once again brimming.

***

The clatter of horse's hooves treading on the stony ground of Hampton Court Palace drew Bess's attention away from the castle's front doors. A pair of black carthorses stomped by the start of the path leading away from the castle. George stood beside them, patting their sides and murmuring to them. Bess smiled at the tussled hair that twisted from beneath his cap. Looking to the thick gates that still remained shut, Bess lifted the skirts of her cream summer dress from the ground and strode over to the horses. As she approached, she noticed that behind the blinders, the horses' eyes were wide and white. "Can you not remove those horrid black screens?" she asked.

George turned in surprise and smiled at the young maid. He ran a hand over his untrimmed beard before responding. "No, I cannot," he began with a frown. "They prefer to keep them in the dark. Seems to be quite a trend these days at this castle," George said, voice dropping to a mumble. "Things are getting darker, you know? This whole divorce is no light matter in our land."

Bess's eyes widened. "Now is hardly the place to bring up such matters, George," she rebutted in a hoarse whisper. She cleared her throat. "There is too thick a crowd."

"That is what makes it the perfect time," the lanky man said. "Surely you know something about what troubles plague these palace walls, Bess, being that you are the queen's attendant. Things are amiss in England."

"Perhaps they are..." Bess mumbled in return, wrapping her cloak around her shoulders despite the heat that beat down over her pale skin. For a moment, she pondered confessing to George all that she had learned from Catherine, but the sickening anticipation of betrayal to her queen and a sharp creak from behind stopped her. Bess turned to see the castle gates open. A single man with a slip of paper stood at the threshold, waiting.

He stepped forward and cleared his throat, holding the paper in front of him and squinting down at the black script scrawled across it. "On this day, the twenty-third day of May of the year 1533, the marriage of Catherine of Aragon, princess of Spain by birthright, and our own lord, Great King Henry VIII of England, has been officially dissolved. At this time, the newly titled Princess Dowager of Wales shall be escorted from Hampton Court to reside elsewhere, at Kimbolton Castle."

The man stepped back behind the grand archway, revealing a procession led by Catherine. Holding up her head, encircled by a thin crown of pointed triangular turrets and jewels, the elegant woman stepped forward. Her green velvet dress hugged her thin waist and trailed behind her. Her hands were clasped together in front of her stomach, allowing the shawl covering her arms to drape behind her. With each long stride she took, Catherine's matching veil drifted across small billows of air.

Catherine's ladies in waiting and servants followed close behind. Their heads hung low, with the exception of one olive-toned woman wearing a deep burgundy dress that swept side to side with each confident step. This woman smiled while she watched Catherine stride from the palace for the final time. Bess scowled at the mere sight of the woman and weaved through the crowd to the end of the castle's front pathway. As Catherine passed, she was the first to dip into a low courtesy. The former queen continued to push her way towards her carriage, and the crowd respectfully followed Bess's lead.

Leaving all those present bowed before her, Catherine and her company arrived at the foot of the carriage. George bowed and offered a steady arm to the queen. Bracing herself against George's forearm, Catherine climbed into the carriage, knees creaking as she struggled to lift the heavy weight of her dress upwards. Bess rose and rushed over to the carriage, gathering the hefty skirts into her arms and holding them as Catherine took a seat in the padded, enclosed carriage. Once again, Bess curtsied to Catherine. The young maid received a nod in return as Catherine continued to maintain her noble silence.

"Let us step back," George said to Bess alone. The two moved away. Four of Catherine's ladies followed her into the carriage, taking their places beside Catherine on cushioned seats. The driver jumped into the front with ease and gathered the reins in his left hand. He whistled and smacked the bottom of the horse to his right. With a snort, the horse leapt forward.

The people rose and watched as the carriage rolled away from Hampton Court Palace, its wooden wheels churning up dust. The bright coach careened over loose stones and rocks. Bess saw through its windows that Catherine sat straight, shoulders pushed back regally. Bess covered her mouth in fear of letting out a cry as she watched her queen leave down the road. Hearing a scoff behind her, she turned to see the woman in red twirl and retreat back towards the castle, leading the remaining group of ladies with her. Bess felt a reassuring hand take hold of her upper arm. She looked up to where George stood, a forced smile highlighting his cheeks. Bess nodded to him sadly and looked past his face to catch a final glimpse of Catherine as the land closed to conceal her carriage.

Beheaded

AN UNCAPPED VIAL

Blinded by the cloth, Anne felt a shiver shoot down her spine as the harsh blade of the sword pressed against the nape of her narrow neck. From where the cold curve of the edge cut against her skin, the chill spread and stilled her shaking body. Her pulse pumped in her ears, blocking out the dull voices of those speaking on her behalf. Heavy boots stomped away, and Anne felt the wooden boards of the platform shake against her feet. A muffled voice spoke in her ear, and Anne struggled to understand the man's message. Perhaps it was not the low volume, but rather the echoing of Anne's rapid heart pulsing against her own eardrums that impaired her understanding. Nudging her with his elbow, the man repeated himself. "Last words?" he questioned. Anne nodded, bringing her hands together in front of her chest.

She opened her mouth to speak, but her voice faltered.

***

The trouble had begun just a year ago, in late January of the year 1535. So soon into her marriage, Anne had proven herself to be far more successful than Catherine, her predecessor. She had produced a child but a few months after being wed to England's king. Elizabeth was a darling daughter, with wispy red and brown hair darker than even her mother's. The child was quiet, behaving like a young queen even as a tripping toddler. Anne was in love with her child, even more so than she was with her haughty husband Henry, or with her glorious life as queen.

Still, the king longed for a male heir, and Anne was indeed ready to satisfy the king's desire. The palace was alive with excitement, preparing for another healthy child. But by the end of January, as snow was dusting the cobblestone grounds of Hampton Court, Anne had failed to produce a thriving boy.

Her first attempt had emerged as a pale, ghostly boy, white skin smooth and cold. The nurses had handed the still baby to Anne, who wrapped the fragile body against her chest, hoping her heartbeat might spark some spirit to re-enter her son's body. He lay motionless in her arms. Anne had rapidly gone through emotions, sadness transforming into rampant anger as she banished the nurses from their positions. Nonetheless, her handmaid Bess's efficiency and consistent silence satisfied Anne. The attendant was allowed to remain to help ease the queen – until the failure of Anne's second attempt to bear a boy into the royal line.

The second child faired no better, his life ending just weeks after Anne's pregnancy began. Bess had been making her way to her mistress's privy chambers, extra blankets and quilts piled high underneath her chin. As she rounded into the base court of the palace, she noticed a lone figure collapsed near the foot of the square's marble fountain. It was not uncommon for beggars to sit there with their empty wooden cups. Nor was it strange for a passerby to glance upon a drunkard sprawled over the wooden steps, his socks ripped and his shorts pulled up high around his thighs. But the sun had set this wintery day in January, and Bess knew the consequence of this weather would be the stranger's life.

She glanced around the yard and saw that the other members of court had retreated to the warmth of their chambers long ago. Bess stopped in her path to Anne's apartments. "Good cheer!" she called out, watching the heat of her breath bounce against the chill of the air. "I say, good cheer!" she repeated. When she received no response, Bess warily made her way through the snow to the woman. "It is a mighty cold night to lay against these steps, madam," she prompted from a distance. "Perhaps you ought to make your way to an inn. I am not a wealthy woman, but I will pay for a ride into town and a night of warmth if you are in need."

The woman remained unmoving.

Bess tucked her blankets under one arm and hurried to shake the sleeping stranger's shoulder. The woman stirred and struggled to open her frosty eyes. They widened at the sight of Bess, and her hand, which had been clutched over her stomach, reached to hold on to the maid's dress. Bess jumped back, dropping her blankets. "Leave me be!"

"Bess..." the voice croaked out. Bess startled, recognizing the rasp of Anne's voice.

"Your Majesty...?" she questioned, and the figure let out a responsive sob. Bess knelt by the woman and brushed the wild hair back from her face. Bess recognized her slight nose and thin eyebrows and dropped to her knees beside her queen. She scrambled to retrieve the fallen quilts from the ground and tugged them over her mistress. "What became of you, My Lady?" she asked, wrapping the now damp blankets around her trembling figure. Anne's lips were turning as dark a blue as that of her navy dress. "We must remove you from the cold."

Bess called for help, then watched as candlelight appeared in the windows surrounding the courtyard. As she waited for assistance, she coaxed Anne from her place on the steps, decorated with sooty snow. The two began to hobble towards Anne's chambers. Bess turned her head, let out a desperate gasp, loosening her hold on the frozen queen. Behind them in the gathered snow, a patch of pink gave way to a trail of darker red blotches. Bess looked down in alarm to a stain of blood lacing Anne's dress, and droplets of blood behind them that fell with each step they took.

Servants, maids, and noblemen alike rushed into the courtyard, all dressed in thick bedclothes and ruffled expressions. "Who do you hold, Bess?" a voice called out from beneath the stone arch.

Bess shook her head and tore her eyes from the sight. "Q-Queen Boleyn," she stuttered. A few of the noblemen began to murmur, failing to move and offer help, but arching their necks for a better view. Male guards and servants rushed forward to support the queen. Bess motioned with frenzied gestures for her friends to gather. Two women tightened their shawls around their shoulders and left the warm doorway, joining Bess in the brisk wind. "She is very hurt," Bess said and gestured to the blood that was beginning to fade beneath a fresh layer of snow. "Call for the nurses, bring fresh blankets and clothes, and send a messenger to wake the king. Something is wrong with his queen."

The other maids glanced around Bess and covered their mouths in shock. They linked arms and scurried off towards the palace, their frantic voices echoing through the tall halls. Bess wrapped her shawl around herself and ran to catch up with the men who carried the queen towards her apartments. Just past the base court, they turned left into a dark staircase and rushed to ascend the stone steps.

"Release me..." Anne croaked when the warmth from the fireplace hit her face. The men stopped.

"Do not," Bess cried. "She must be brought to her privy chamber for she is in poor condition." The men nodded and pushed forward, even as Anne's voice grew and she began to writhe in their hold. Once in her chambers, the men placed Anne on her bed and stepped back, watching the queen squirm. "Give the lady privacy, but do not retreat too far," Bess said as she darted into the room and prepared a cloth to dab at the sweat across Anne's face. "We may need you in a moment."

The guards exited the room as a nurse rushed inside. She was short and pale-faced, having just been awakened in the late hours of the night. She pushed back her disheveled hair and pulled at the robe around her waist. "I hear that Queen Boleyn is of poor health," she said. Bess's two friends, arms filled with blankets and linen smocks, shoved past the nurse to Anne's bedside. The nurse looked across the room to where Anne lay, breathless. She dropped her robe and snatched a smock from the nearest maid, taking the casual dress and wrapping it around her waist as a makeshift apron. "Please," the nurse said, waving at the excess company. "Leave the queen. Such a crowded room could only make her illness worsen by the minute."

Bess nodded to her friends, thanking them and closing the door behind them. "She has been pregnant these past weeks," Bess said to the concerned nurse. "I worry for the child's safety."

"As do I," the nurse replied, urging Anne to lower herself onto her back. The queen buckled, hands pressed over her stomach. "Please excuse me, Highness," said the nurse as she hiked up Anne's skirts. The nurse took a sharp inhale of air and stumbled back. "Dear me..." she breathed out.

"Good God, madam, what is it?" Bess attempted to take a step forward. The nurse thrust out an arm to stop her and ushered Bess to the side.

"I am afraid the child is lost," the nurse murmured to Bess alone.

"Lost? As with the last?"

"This child no longer lives. Her Majesty's body has miscarried the young fetus."

"What is wrong?" Anne cried out from her bed. Her head lashed to the side to see the two women whispering. "Is the child affected?"

The maid and the nurse glanced to one another before making their way to Anne's side. Bess gripped Anne's hand while the nurse wiped a cool cloth across her sweating forehead. "It is the child," the nurse said. "It no longer lives."

Anne let out a terrifying cry, one that made Bess's eyes water and the fire in the room flicker. The nurse said no more, but shuffled to the end of the bed and prodded Anne's legs apart. The next few hours, Bess sat at Anne's head, stroking her delicate forehead. She did not see the queen's brown eyes turn darker and darker, black seeping in with her anger. As the night came to a close and the sun began to slip through the clear cracks of the chamber's windows, Anne's body relaxed, and she allowed her eyes to clamp shut. The nurse sighed and looked to Bess. "The child..." she began. "He would have been a boy."

Anne's eyes flashed open. "Twice!" she yelled, directing a glare at Bess. "Twice now I have lost a young boy in your presence. You curse me just as your last mistress did from our first meeting on. Leave my chambers and dare not to return."

Bess squealed as the woman batted at her with her spindly fingers. She clutched her chest and ran from the room, fighting the urge to faint at the sight of the blood-covered, curled-up being that lay in the nurse's hands. From her quarters, she gathered her belongings and sent word in to town that she needed a way of getting to Kimbolton Castle. By the time the sun sat right above the palace's towers, Bess was trotting her way to report news of the events to her exiled friend and former queen, Catherine of Aragon.

***

Back in her apartments, Anne fell into her damp bed and huffed in anger.

"My Queen?" the nurse prodded, still holding the miscarried fetus in her hands.

"Leave and take the boy with you," Anne hollered before she buried her face in her pillow. "I cannot stand to see him." With a sigh, the nurse left.

Trouble continued to brew. With Bess gone and her ladies in waiting offering nothing but pity and pathetic gossip, Anne was left alone in her chambers with none to watch over her. Throughout the time that passed, Anne sent messengers to town, searching for a new attendant to serve and entertain her. But each maid that came and went only worked to anger the queen, provoking her frustration. As new servants circulated through her apartments each week, Anne's reputation began to spread through the land. Even prior to her arrival to the throne, many knew Anne and thought low of her. Rumors held that she had known many men before Henry, that lovers had come and gone. It was common knowledge that Anne sought after power and wealth. Why else would she have involved herself with the sixth Earl of Northumberland, Henry Percy? He had been a rude, military man of harsh tastes and few words, bar those of criticism. His attitude clashed with that of headstrong Anne, their opinions on religious reform and the legal necessities of marriage being quite opposite one another. Yet, he had been smitten with the olive-skinned lady, and the manipulative mistress had not been opposed to the influential man's advances. It was only when a greater man, a king no less, caught Anne's eye that her relations to Percy had been cut off. Anne was known to be a woman of such vile and stubborn character, that even the poorest of maids would only offer her services to the queen with great reluctance.

So Anne found herself with time to spare, moping about her

room when she was unable to coax Henry out of his to take her into town or dress her in elegant regalia. As her lack of a son continued to frustrate her, theories and schemes began to swim in Anne's head. Everyone knew that if she could not produce a male heir for the king, she would be cast aside. Her background and poor status with the courts were no help in keeping her in the castle. The sole idea of being forced to leave the palace and her marriage with the king was not terrible to Anne. The two royals fought often, and even if Anne were to be divorced, she had her ways of assuring that she would be treated well outside of the palace. Regardless of marital status, Anne had methods of influencing and maneuvering the king's manners in ways that few others could comprehend.

Still, there was one thing that Anne could not stand if she were to be exiled. The next eldest in the line of Tudors was not her own daughter, her beloved Elizabeth, but Mary, daughter of Catherine of Aragon. To an extent, Anne pitied the ex-queen. Anne had, after all, made sure that she produced no male heir. It had all been part of Anne's plan to gain a royal position by her Henry. However, Catherine was far too snobbish for Anne's tastes, and Anne maintained a great grudge against her. The woman had been betrothed and married to her love, Henry, keeping his potential affection for Anne locked in a heart of solid steel. Anne's distaste for Catherine had grown as time passed, and she watched her Henry become miserable in a marriage to such a controlling and customary woman. These sentiments made firing Catherine's former maid all the more easy. It also made Anne's plan to dispose of the older woman's daughter far less maniacal in her eyes. Were Anne to be divorced as the last had been, she could not stand to watch Mary take the throne. The Boleyn bloodline must carry on through history.

***

One early spring morning, Anne finalized a plan as she sat in the gardens behind the palace, watching the gardeners trim the broken branches from the fruit trees. Sitting on a wooden bench, Anne waited for Mary to take her usual stroll through to the pond gardens, her favorite sector of the extravagant grounds. At half past twelve, Mary rounded the red wall of the palace with her small company of ladies and ducked through the metal gate fastened to the stone wall surrounding the greens. Her arms swayed by her sides, the billowing cuffs of her dress sleeves waving behind her. A casual grey scarf hid her hair, keeping stray strands back from her face. Anne leaned forward to watch the young princess make her way down the gravel path. As she neared, she raised her hand in greeting. "Mary, darling!" she called.

The young woman startled, her hands moving to her chest to cover the rose medallion resting there. Seeing Anne, she let out a deep breath, though her shoulders remained tense. "Queen Boleyn," she said, dipping into a curtsy. Those by her sides also blushed and let themselves fall into deep curtsies. Mary bent her legs but kept her head high, maintaining eye contact with the queen. "What chance has allowed our paths to cross this afternoon?" she said.

Anne stood from her seat and offered a fur-clad arm to Mary. "I thought we might take a stroll alone," Anne said, nodding at the still-bent ladies. They smiled and raised themselves, and then turned down another path to give the pair privacy. Mary glanced after them and, with great hesitancy, looped her arm through Anne's. The two picked up a leisurely pace towards the pond gardens. "I have been so lonely these passing days," Anne began. "With your poor mother sent away, bless her soul, I can see that you too spend many hours alone." Mary nodded, though less in agreement and far more in hopes of unraveling the queen's motives for this chat. "I have seen that you are a fine young lady. In fact, your father tells me that you have mastered multiple languages."

Anne's eyebrows rose.

"Why yes," Mary replied, removing her arm from Anne's hold as they arrived at the pond gardens. "I have studied language, music, and dance since I was but four years old. My mother insisted I be well learned, and that resolve has served me sound thus far." Mary gazed out across the gardens, resting her arms between the metal spikes of the fence.

"Of course, I am certain," said Anne. "It fascinates me that a woman of your age and background should thrive so in her education."

"Background, My Lady?" Mary questioned, not moving her gaze away from the sculptures arching their backs in the center of the ponds before her.

"Your parents did separate when you were still young, my dear." Anne sent a sympathetic smile Mary's way, and placed a hand on the young woman's shoulders. Mary shifted as if leaning forward to see more of the gardens. Anne's hand fell back to her side. "No longer does a mother reside with you to guide you through these transitions into womanhood. No one remains at home to prompt you in discussion and thought." Anne straightened her back and said, "This is why I would like to invite you for afternoon refreshments tomorrow in my privy chambers."

Mary turned to look at Anne. "Queen Boleyn," she rushed to respond. "You are a busy woman with many official duties, and I do not wish to intrude upon – "

"There would be no intrusion at all," Anne retorted. Mary began to speak, but the queen cut her off. "I insist. During the fourth hour of the afternoon, I will send a man to bring you to my apartments. We shall drink and dine and discuss. Does this suit you?"

"It does," Mary said. She ducked into a half bow and looked away. "Thank you for the invitation. It is an honor."

"It shall be my pleasure." Anne backed away as Mary swung open the black gate to the gardens and strode inside, turning left behind a hedge and disappearing from Anne's sight. Anne smirked to herself. She whirled around and strode back towards the castle, her black underskirts swishing and kicking up a small cloud of dust.

***

An oval table sat at the end of the hall, far away from the tall rectangular windows at the entrance. A regal set of items rested on its polished brown surface. Two silver goblets, each traced with intricate trails of golden pigments mimicking the growth of vines outside the palace windows, sat atop the table's shining surface. Bowls with handles fit for slender fingers were off to the side, deep basins filled with sugar cubes, salted nuts, and seeds of varying assortments. Small pots enclosed warm fruit, cooked pineapple and baked chunks of apples. Altogether, the collection released a pleasant, comforting smell into the air of the stuffy palace.

Anne sat, straight-backed, on a wooden chair beside the table. Slippers removed, she rested her feet on the crafted curved bars intertwining to and from the legs of the table. She glanced to the grand clock that sat on the mantle above the fireplace and watched the tapered finger of the minute hand tick until it pointed up at the hand-painted ceiling high above her head. With a smile, Anne listened to the clock's gentle chimes and reached over the table to grasp the tall neck of the goblet closest to her. Holding it by her fingertips, she sipped from the cup and turned her eyes to the door. After placing it down once again, Anne dropped a sugar cube into her mouth, leaned back, and waited for Mary's arrival.

Moments later, a door at the end of the hall creaked open. The footman, dressed in puffy trousers and a structured blue jacket, stepped through the threshold. "Princess Mary, daughter of the distinguished King Henry himself, comes to meet with our lady and queen."

Anne stood. "Allow her entry."

The man bowed deep, rose, placed a hand in the fold between his jacket buttons, and stepped to the side, leaving the doorway open. Mary entered and glanced around the room. She caught Anne's eye and looked down, taking up her skirts and dipping into a curtsy. "My Queen," she said with a hint of distaste flicking from the verge of her voice.

"Mary, so lovely to meet with you this brisk afternoon." Anne returned the young woman's curtsy with a drawn out nod, a smile fixed across her dark face. She motioned to the arrangement beside her, hand sweeping over the oval table and the two chairs adjacent to it. "Please, come sit with me."

Mary glanced out the rectangular windows at the vibrant gardens beyond before she turned to Anne and crossed the open space. She arrived at where Anne stood, stone still, and glanced at the older woman before sitting down on the chair. Anne too sat and pushed one goblet to Mary. "It is a rather chilly day out, is it not?"

"I suppose so, considering the season," Mary responded. "Might I ask why we are meeting in this grand hall rather than in your chambers, as you proposed?" Mary fiddled with the base of the tall silver cup.

"Henry did leave our room early this morning for his day out with the horses, and being unaware of our afternoon meeting, the servants did put out the fire in the room. It was dreadful in there," Anne said, rubbing her bare arms. "Here, the sun warms the floors and keeps the room at a pleasant temperature. It seemed more fitting to meet where we can be comfortable."

"Yes, I understand." Mary fidgeted in her seat. She pulled the fur wrap closer to her body. Again she looked around the bare room. One of Anne's ladies in waiting had wandered into the room, appearing lost. She glanced at the pair before she fumbled into a curtsy and hurried back out. The footman still waiting just outside the door nodded at the woman. Mary considered calling for him to retrieve the woman before being interrupted by the queen.

"Are you all right, dear?" Anne asked, the smile slipping from her face and a look of concern molding to her features. "Drink up! The wine is quite a fresh taste, and will warm your bones in but a moment."

"Thank you," Mary said. She picked up her cup and placed it against her red lips, taking a light sip. Anne followed suit. Only a tiny trickle of wine passed her mouth and slid down her throat.

Mary scrunched her nose and swallowed thickly. "Why, it does have quite a strong taste..."

"There is a bite to the drink," Anne confessed, watching Mary as she nodded in agreement. Anne popped a sugar cube into her mouth and leaned back against the ribs of her chair. "How go your studies?" she asked upon Mary's silence.

Mary took another sip of her wine before cupping her hands around the cool goblet. "They have been challenging as of late," she responded, taking a crunchy almond. Biting it in two, she remained silent while chewing.

"How so?" Anne prompted.

Mary swallowed and took another sip of wine to wash the rough salt from her mouth. "My instructors do say that I have become proficient, and perhaps even fluent, in both the French and Spanish languages. However, my language instructor hopes to teach me some of the Greek language, and I have been struggling to comprehend it. Also, I find little use for these languages. I feel my time is better spent practicing my dances for coming performances in court. Dedicating such a great amount of time to language draws time away from that which I can spend with my art and religion."

"But these languages are what shall make you a powerful leader," Anne said. "They allow communication to flourish between all people."

"Belief and religion allow communication to flourish," Mary combatted. "Translators will always exist in plenty, but it is who we are that connects us to the rest of the world." Mary gave Anne a smirk and took another almond, once again sipping from her cup to rinse away the salt and taste left behind.

Anne mirrored Mary's haughty look as she noticed the young lady's goblet was near empty. "I suppose you make a good point. But do beliefs not seem more sincere when coming from one's own mouth? How can you expect a man or woman of any stature to believe your ideals when you cannot even speak in their own tongue?"

"When the religion is right, such trivial matters hold no standing."

"Perhaps you believe so, but society, the great people of this town, do not see as such." Anne ate another sugar cube as Mary took a handful of almonds. She ate the nuts and then finished off her drink.

"Perchance..." Mary responded and leaned back to rest against her chair. She twisted in an attempt to rest in a more comfortable position. "But it is not the common folk who need persuading," she said. Mary glanced to the open door at the end of the hall. "Good sir," she called, forcing herself to straighten in her seat. "Mightn't I have a pillow to sit upon? My back does ache so."

The footman poked his head inside the doorway. The man stood with one hand gripping the doorframe. "I shall retrieve one right away, My Lady," he responded and the man scurried off. Mary returned her attention to Anne.

"I believe your point to be untrue," Anne retorted, watching Mary slump. The queen grinned to herself and continued. "The common folk are the ones who support a person of royalty. To earn their respect and response, one must conduct oneself in a kindly, respectful fashion at all times. Only then can communications be successful."

Mary leaned forward, her wrap falling from her stooped shoulders. She placed an elbow on the table and shoved her now empty cup to the side with a clatter. "Such a mindset has not proven very useful in your own case..." she muttered and reached for another almond. As she did so, her elbow gave way and Mary crumpled downwards, her torso twisting as she lowered herself to the floor. Her eyes sluggishly moved in search of Anne before they closed.

With a satisfied chuckle, Anne stood and strode to where Mary was now sleeping, her plan taking effect. She pulled Mary's warm body to the side and laid her back on the floor. Parting her skirts and kneeling beside Mary, Anne watched the breath hiss out of Mary's nose as her heartbeat slowed. Mary's head rolled to the side. Her cold, pale cheek rested against the floor. Her lips parted as her jaw slackened.

"How naïve you really are, Mary," Anne said, talking to the sleeping girl before her. She used her fingernails to brush Mary's dull, wavy hair away from her face. "You are so much like your mother in that way. She too knew little about the true workings of the world." Anne stretched up to pull one of the small jars from the tabletop beside her. Opening it, she extracted a thin bottle filled with a thick grey liquid. She returned to Mary's side and grasped the girl's chin, pulling her face to point towards the ceiling. Anne tugged the cork from the bottle and leaned close to Mary, whispering, "And now, you get to face the fate that I so wished – "

"Anne!"

Startled, Anne fell back and away from Mary's body.

"What are you doing?" the voice boomed. Anne scrambled to

stand and looked up to where Henry – escorted by Anne's own lady and the footman, who carried a pillow by its tassels – stood. Henry had made his way halfway across the room, and waited beside the fireplace. Hands gripping his sides, he glared down at the sight before him with dark eyes. "What ails the poor girl so?"

"She collapsed, the young thing," Anne responded, voice unsteady.

"Sirrah," Henry boomed and turned to face the footman. "Why are you not yet rushing to retrieve assistance? Off with you." The man spun on his heel and rushed off down the corridor, quickening footsteps fading away fast. Henry turned his attention back to his nervous wife, who had inched away from Mary's body. "What truly happened?" he insisted while glaring at Anne. "Answer me!"

"As I did say, My King: the girl, she collapsed," Anne answered. "I was helping to – "

"Why then did you loom with such hatred in your eyes over her figure?" he said. "And what do you hold in your hand?" Henry moved forward. She closed her hand around the bottle in a desperate attempt to conceal its existence.

"Nothing, Majesty." Anne folded her hands in front of her and bowed her head as Henry approached. "Just a simple container of sugar."

"Allow me to see this sugar, then." Anne hesitated. "This instance, Anne!"

Anne pried open her fingers and revealed the bottle, its murky liquid swimming around the clear vial. Henry snatched the bottle away. Anne bit the inside of her lip, struggling to maintain a blank face.

Henry examined the bottle. His eyes widened in realization when he watched the contents of the bottle slosh back and forth. Hands shaking, he tucked the vial into his waistband and reached with both hands to grasp Anne's arms. His hands dug into her bare skin and she clenched her eyes shut. "Anne," he said, his voice fearful. Anne opened her eyes to see that his were filled with anger and concern. "You display the signs of a witch. What crime did you inflect upon my eldest daughter?"

His gaze tightened along with his grip, and Anne squealed in response. "Nothing, truly. She collapsed as we – "

"These lies are unacceptable." Henry's brow creased. Anne let out a low cry. He released her and began to pace back and forth. One hand pulled at the tip of his short beard while the other rubbed his forehead in thought. Throwing one last disappointed look to Anne, he called out across the room. "You, madam!" He strode towards the woman.

The lady in waiting came forward in fright to meet the king. "Your M-Majesty?"

"Find the footman and make clear the urgency of this situation. A nurse and company must be fetched to care for Princess Mary as soon as is possible." The woman gave a short curtsy and ran from the room. "As for you," the king said, turning back to Anne. "You shall be taken to the cells and be charged for plots of murder against me and my great family." Anne gasped and dropped to the ground. Henry stomped towards his queen, each of his footsteps matching the quick and weighty beats of Anne's nervous heart.

***

"Last words?" the man repeated once more, voice taut.

"Yes," Anne managed to respond.

"Before Anne Boleyn, queen of our great land, is executed on this nineteenth day of May in the Lord's year of 1536 for assorted crimes against our Great King, she will speak." The man removed the blade from her neck. Anne heard its tip dig into the wooden boards beneath her.

She took a breath that sent yet another round of shaking

51

through her body. "Good Christian people," she began. She straightened her back and turned her head where she believed the crowd to be. "I have not come here to preach; I have come here to die, for according to the law and by the law I am judged to die, and I cannot speak to prevent this." Anne imagined Henry sitting above the crowd, listening to her speech. She lowered her head to where the crowd lingered. "I have come here to accuse no man, but rather to pray that God save King Henry and send him to long reign over you good English people." Anne held back a sneer. "There never was a gentler, nor a more merciful, prince. To me he was ever a good, gentle, and sovereign lord." She lowered her head and felt the warmth of the wet cloth covering her eyes grow heavier. "And thus I take my leave of the world and of you all, and I heartily desire you all to pray for me."

Anne held her shoulders back, her head high, leaving her long neck exposed. The executioner tugged the sword from the wood paneling. His footsteps collided against the ground, this time the steps falling far slower than the beat of Anne's heart. Hands clasped together before her, Anne could swear she heard the sword lift through the humid air to balance above the executioner's head. She took a swift inhale and with the trembling exhale, the sword flew and cut through the witch's dainty neck.

Died

MY MODEST MAIDEN

Henry paced the back halls of Hampton Court Palace, passing by his familiar collection of tapestries that hung heavily from the walls. He reached the end of the gallery and whipped around. With his hands clenched by his sides, he stomped back through the hall. He passed extravagant parades depicted in gold and red threads; angry market places sewn together with thick, dark strings; and even crowds cheering at coronations, the people's hard helmets outlined in deep hues of purple and brown.

Henry reached the end of the corridor and halted. Before him hung a tapestry, leaning left due to the hefty weight upon the weak knobby nails. Hercules, the great hero himself, boasted across the carpet-like material, seven statues gracing its surface. Henry skimmed over the depictions of Hercules in envy: Hercules pushing down an upwards lion; the hero wrestling enemies to the ground with his bare hands; even the man, hands extended to the sky above, conversing with cherubs as they floated down from Heaven to grace his presence. Henry tilted his head and held his hands over his rounded stomach, his head throbbing as he squinted his eyes to focus on the mocking images above him.

"Useless!" he yelled and lashed out to smack the tapestry. Its surface wavered back and forth under the impact. Henry glared at it, fists once again held tight at his sides. He huffed in frustration and rushed to exit the hall, finding a group of nervous servants waiting outside the high doors.

"My Lord?" a footman asked.

"Leave me be," the ruler snapped in return. He strode through the group and shouldered past the man who stumbled backwards and raised a hand in protest, but received no response from the frustrated king. "Does my wife still remain in her chambers?" he called, not bothering to shorten his stride or cease his walking to wait for a response.

"She does, King Henry," the footman responded. "Would you like me to take you to her?"

"I hardly need a man such as yourself to lead me through my own courts, sirrah," Henry bit back and retreated.

Henry strode through the courtyards of the palace with his robe, embellished with gold thread and edged with small ornaments, swishing behind him. Courtiers bowed their heads in waves as he marched past, but the king did not bother to wave a hand to raise them. Within the minute, Henry reached the yard's apartments and paused before the wooden door. He placed a wide hand on its center, considering his next move. Taking his other adorned hand, clad in thick rings and bands of silver and gold, he rapped on the door three times.

The door swung open, away from Henry, and he let his hands drop to his sides. A timid maid stood before him. She looked up to her king and, catching his glance, ducked into a curtsy that skirted far too close to the floor. "My Lord," she said hastily, gesturing inwards. Henry nodded, gathered himself, and walked into the room.

His heartbeat skipped in terror when he caught sight of his wife, lying back in their marital bed. Her face was framed by wispy blonde hair, tangled and matted down by the sweat glistening on her forehead. Her eyes were closed, but not in rest, her brow wrinkled in concentration. Her hands clenched around her sheets, her knuckles turning whiter than her pale face under the pressure. Perhaps the most devastating facet of the image laid before Henry was the soft wheeze that his sick wife drew in through her dry, parted lips. *Oh, good Lord,* Henry thought, gazing at his wife. *What have I done?* Henry cautiously approached, noting his wife's fragility. He removed his hat and held it against his chest. The queen let out a shuddering breath, which vibrated throughout her entire body, causing her arms to shake and her lips to tremble.

Those surrounding the bed bowed as Henry drew nearer. A doctor wearing dark robes and carrying strange instruments in his hands withdrew. Henry saw the dampness of the bed sheets, their light surface blending with his wife's pale skin. "Oh Jane," he breathed out, handing his hat to a servant. Henry looked down at his suffering queen in despair.

With great care, Jane opened her eyes. They swam for a moment before they focused and swiveled to the direction of Henry's voice. Seeing his face, she relaxed her shoulders back against the pillows padded underneath her. "My King..." she whispered, releasing her tight grip and extending a hand to Henry. "What a gift it is to see you during this time." Henry took Jane's hand. Her fingers were lanky, and they held a tremor. Henry raised his wife's moist hand to his lips and gave it a squeeze in hope of prompting some strength to return, but the tremble remained. "Were I of better health, I would rise and meet your solid gaze, my love," she continued, her voice dropping off into a fit of soft coughs. A maid rushed forward to dab at her forehead, staying until Jane waved her off with a twitch of her fingers.

"I am certain of it," Henry said. He unhooked his robe and handed it to a footman behind him. Again looking at Jane, Henry felt his heart thumping against his heavy chest, guilt clawing at his mind all the while. "Seeing your state, it only seems fitting that I come down to you and meet your eye." Henry sat down upon the edge of her bed, and Jane curled her lips into a smile. Using the little strength that remained in her arms, she pushed herself up a few inches to meet Henry's gaze. His dark green eyes were strangely comforting to the gentle woman. The thought brought a tint, a faint blush, to Jane's cheeks.

"How kind you are," she responded. Jane placed her hand atop Henry's. "How come preparations for the christening? How fares Edward?"

Edward. Henry fought to keep his expression firm, thinking of his thriving son whom his wife had yet to cradle in her arms. "He fares well, though he cries often for his mother."

Jane's smile sagged. "I do wish I were of better health to care for the boy." She shook her head and squeezed Henry's hand. "Tell me about him."

Henry gave an unsettled laugh and tried to smile at his wife. "He is quite a handsome boy," he began. "His eyes are bright, like your own. They are quite captivating, for their color leans towards grey with each day that does pass. But his cheeks remain constant. They are rosy, as if always dusted in a veil of powder. When he weeps, the color spreads up towards his ears, and they too glow, shining against his soft tufts of hair. He is swept up in preparations now, but he shall be brought to your chambers so that the christening may begin."

Jane's eyes glistened with tears. "He sounds absolutely glorious."

"He is, my dear," Henry responded. He wiped Jane's tears away

60

with a clumsy swipe of his thick thumb.

Jane gripped his hand. "I look forward to seeing him this afternoon." She allowed her eyes to flutter closed once again, and her body slipped back down below the sheets in relaxation.

Henry looked down at her, pity lining his countenance. "He should be returned to us within the hour." Henry reached down to sweep back a damp strand of hair that had fallen across Jane's face. "The ceremonies will begin then."

"So soon?" she questioned, opening her eyes. "I am hardly in a state to be receiving my son. I am not currently fit to receive courtiers for the christening." Her hand went slack in Henry's.

Henry stood and looked around the room. "We shall prepare you. Shall we not?" He spread his arms around him, and those in the room nodded with vigor. Henry took the encouragement and turned to the footman nearest him, who still stood clutching his hat and robe. "Put those dressings away for a time and fetch me a basin."

"Certainly, Your Highness," he replied, passing Henry's clothing on to another before rushing from the room with another servant at his heels.

"You, madam," Henry ordered, pointing at a young woman. "Find Queen Jane her attire and prepare it." The maid scurried off, and Henry continued to deal out instructions while Jane lay back in her bed. Once the footman returned with a small tub of water, with the basin balanced on his hip, Henry helped to prepare Jane for their son's christening.

Henry reached under Jane's arms and hoisted her up into a sitting position. He waved his hands, face flustered, at the many maids and men that attempted to help him. He sat beside Jane once more, allowing her to clutch onto his arm and lean her feeble weight against him. With fumbling hands, Henry smoothed Jane's hair back and set to work washing her face. He took up a cloth and dunked it into the basin before wiping it across Jane's gleaming forehead and flushed cheeks. He ran the cloth over her neck, covered in sweat from a morning of restlessness. Henry felt her shiver, and he pulled the bed sheets up around her waist. Henry placed the cloth down and reached for Jane's hairbrush. He held it and hesitated.

Jane let out a meek giggle. Her demeanor softened, and she reached to tug the brush from his hand. "Perhaps it might benefit all if Margaret were to attend to my hair, My King."

The timid maid who had admitted Henry to the room scurried forward. "How might I be of help, Lady Jane?" Her hands fidgeted by her sides.

"My hair," Jane said. "Might you tame its knots and pin it upwards so that I might wear my white head cover and veil?"

"Yes, My Queen." The maid stepped close beside her. Jane forced a feeble smile and lifted her head. The young woman took Jane's light twists of hair in her hands and pulled the brush through the tangles gathered by the base of Jane's head. Henry sat back, a feeling of helplessness again settling over him. He watched her hair being smoothed out, the damp texture disappearing between the hairs of the brush. The maid spent a few minutes removing the snarls before she scurried off to the dresser to find the queen's outfitting. Henry turned to face Jane again, a sad smile pulling the corner of his lips upwards when he saw how gently Jane's light hair framed her face. He opened his mouth to speak, but paused as Margaret returned with white accessories draped over her thin arms.

"Is this the piece you spoke of, Your Highness?" asked Margaret, holding out her arms.

"Oh yes. It is divine," Jane said with a breathy exhale, taking in the pure material in fascination.

Margaret nodded, but did not step forward. "...My Lady? I

cannot wrap your hair inside the headpiece while you rest against your pillows."

"Of course, yes," Jane answered, glancing around the room. She caught sight of a chair nearby, next to her dresser and mirror. "Henry, my love?" she questioned, catching his attention.

"I... what?" Henry shook his head to clear his thoughts and looked down to Jane. She held out her arms and placed one hand on Henry's shoulder. He scarcely felt the light hand resting atop his shoulder, and he narrowed his eyes again in frustration. How had he allowed his poor wife, a maiden so sweet and lively, to become so fragile?

Jane removed her bed sheets from across her front, using her legs to push them away. "I beg your assistance. Might you lift me and carry me to that chair?" Henry looked over to where the chair sat, and his heart dropped.

He reached down to the frail figure spread out on the bed. He picked her up and held her against his chest. Jane let out a sigh and leaned her head against Henry's cheek while he made his way to the chair. He placed her down, standing beside her so that she might hold steady to his hand for stability. "Thank you, dear," she said. Jane tilted her head up to smile at the king.

"Indeed," he responded, eyes held straight to the wall in fear of the image of his failing wife holding his eye and abating his heart once more.

Margaret, noticing the cease in conversation, approached and took Jane's hair in her hands. Once again brushing it through, she pulled her hair backwards from base to tip. She twisted the smooth hair until it wrapped into itself and folded against the queen's head. Holding the bun tightly against Jane's head with one hand, Margaret pulled out the headpiece from her apron. In one swift movement, the maid tugged the white cap over Jane's hair, pulling its elongated sides down behind her ears. She pushed the wispy hairs floating around Jane's neck up into the tight-fitting wrap and moved back to the bed to find Jane's veil.

She turned to approach the queen once again, but was interrupted by a knock that sounded against the chamber's door. The maid paused and all heads turned. A servant swung open the door, and a courtier with a long moustache drooping over his pouting lips strode inside. The man paused to bow to Henry, one leg bending behind him. "Noble Prince Edward, blessed son of Glorious King Henry, approaches."

"Oh!" Jane gasped. "We must hurry. I must be presentable."

The messenger exited the room. "Retrieve Jane's robes quickly!" Henry said, sending Margaret rushing to the closet to find bright white shawls and lace drapes for her queen. Henry paced behind Jane's chair as Margaret rushed about, other maids pulling Jane to her feet and supporting her by the arms so that Margaret might wrap a long white robe around her. She sat again, gathering herself, and they spread a shawl across her shoulders. Margaret threw Jane's fine veil over her head and, with nimble fingers, hurried to tuck the tattered edges of the veil under Jane's head wrap. The maid lifted the veil a few inches above Jane's neck and back, allowing it to billow downwards and settle across her slender figure, its surface creating a shroud over Jane's pale skin. Another maid rushed forward and presented a goblet of wine to Jane. With a nod from the weary queen, the woman brought the cup to Jane's lips. She took small sips, letting out another sigh as the cup was removed. Margaret popped a sweet into Jane's mouth.

"You look magnificent, Lady Jane," the maid said, a proud look across her face.

Jane, frazzled by all the sudden movement, just stared ahead. "Edward," she began, looking to the door. "Does he come?"

Henry blinked his eyes to clear his blurred vision and stepped forward to Jane's side. "I do believe I hear them approach from down the staircase." Jane nodded and began to fuss with her garbs, pulling her veil around her shoulders more and tucking loose hairs behind her ears. "Do not fret so, my dear," Henry said. "You look exquisite."

Jane smiled. "Thank you, my love." She straightened her back as much as possible and turned her head to face the entrance to her room. Henry grasped the back of Jane's chair, his fingers touching her back. She leaned back against his hand for stability.

The door creaked open, and a procession of courtiers entered the room. They approached, each offering a deep bow to Henry and a kiss on a shaking hand to Jane. Jane gave all men a firm nod, but kept her eyes fixed on the door. Soon, she could hear gentle coos coming through the walls. A select group of her ladies in waiting filed into the room. Jane held her breath, counting off the elegant women lining up in her chambers. Finally, taking up the end of the formal procession, came Margery Horsman. Margery gazed down, grinning, at the child concealed in a great bundle in her arms before she looked up to Jane and followed the procession inwards. "My Queen," Margery said, walking through the parting crowd and dipping into a subtle curtsy.

"Margery." Jane smiled at the woman, and then looked towards where her son lay in her arms. She could not yet see his face, and felt herself begin to sweat once again, this time out of anticipation.

"Prince Edward is doing so well," Margery said. The nurses standing by the entrance nodded their heads in agreement. "He has a healthy cry, and perhaps an even healthier appetite." Jane uncrossed her ankles and placed her feet firmly on the floor, also allowing her shawl to loosen around her shoulders. "Here — I am certain he is just as anxious to see his dear mother as she is to hold him."

Margery lowered the warm bundle into Jane's lap. She pulled her trembling arms together around the boy, salty tears filling her eyes as she took in the sight of her son's red cheeks. His eyes were scrunched shut, and his hands, concealed beneath the lace and extravagance of his christening gown, waved about as if searching for contact. Jane, beaming at the joy in her son's face, inched her hand underneath Edward's blankets to brush her thumb across the prince's palm. His eyes shot open and locked onto Jane's for just a second. Then soft whimpers welled up in his throat and bubbled through his mouth. "He is beautiful..." Jane said.

Henry observed the reunion in solemnity. The boy, with cheeks so rosy, was a stark contrast against the pale, fading color of his mother. The king forced himself to crack a small smile at his wife's wonderment, but the expression did not last. He dropped his shoulders in sadness as he watched the energy drain from Jane's body into that of his son's. "Truly so," Henry responded after a pause. He reached his large hand down to cup his son's soft skull, relieving Jane's tired arms of some of the weight. "Only because he takes after you, Jane," he said in a low voice to his wife.

Jane's face warmed, bringing a temporary glow to her pallid face. She snuggled the boy against her stomach as best she could, then turned to Margery. "I am afraid that my arms already grow so weak. Mightn't we make our way down to the chapel?"

Margery stepped forward, scooping the child out of Jane's arms and holding him tight against her body, his head laid against her shoulder. "Of course, My Queen. Let us proceed to the king's chapel." Courtiers lined up. Jane's ladies in waiting gathered by the door. Margery joined them, and in succession, they proceeded out.

After his son was escorted from the room, Henry returned his attention to Jane, who had wilted against his side for support. "It has been but a few minutes, and my body feels so drained of life."

After a moment's hesitation, Henry stooped down to look Jane in the eye. "My love," he began. His hand moved to rest firmly on her back. "My... our blessed son, whom you brought into this world with such pain and strength, is soon to be recognized in the eyes of God and my kingdom." Henry's spirits wilted more as the truth of the matter sunk in. "Search deep within yourself for that same strength you channeled a few days ago so that we might descend together to the chapel and observe this spectacle."

Jane closed her eyes and small tears dripped through her eyelashes and down her reddened cheeks. Silence followed. Jane sniffed, holding back a deep-chested sob. Henry placed a hand on her shoulder. "It would be shameful not to try," Jane said. "For our beautiful son and for you, My King, I shall try."

Henry looked down at Jane, his expression one of pity and love. "Please," he said to a servant standing at his side. "Bring a litter and the court's strongest men to carry Her Majesty to the ceremonies." The servant nodded and hurried out, his heavy footsteps echoing outside the private chambers.

"Henry," Jane whispered. "Henry, I doubt my ability to make my way down the stairs, unsupported. My legs do give such poor provision for me."

"I shall take you, dear wife."

"My King, the offer is so gracious of you, but I fear that my weight – "

"Oh, Jane," Henry interrupted. "I may not be of my youngest and fittest days, but I can muster the strength to carry your gentle figure out from these walls and down to the courts."

"I do not doubt your strength, but – "

Jane let out a huff as Henry heaved her into his arms. Without a word, he began to stride towards the door. His steps were slow and calculated, his stance as wide as his shoulders to keep himself balanced. Determined to save Jane from any further fear or disruption, he walked with a firm chest and secure arms. "Fetch my robe, hat, and jewels," he barked. "Bring them down behind us."

Jane, realizing Henry's stubbornness in the matter, allowed

herself to relax. She folded her body against Henry's broad chest, curling up against her husband like a fluttering bird into its nest. The tension in her legs released. The royal pair swayed back and forth, making their way down the stone stairs. Henry's breathing was heavy, but with each step downwards, his hold on Jane tightened. Maids and servants followed the pair, watching in worry as the king and queen walked to the lower courts.

"But a few steps left," Henry whispered through a heavy exhale.

Jane murmured against his chest, her dainty fingers clinging to his neck.

Henry stumbled down the last step into the grand courtyard, his face glowing red. He turned his head in search of Jane's litter. In the center of the court, near the edge of the marble fountain and its trickling water, he saw four men waiting by a small, bed-like structure. "Sirrah!" he called across the court, catching the attention of all. "Deliver Queen Jane's litter to me with all haste."

The men jumped into action. They rushed the litter to Henry's side, and the king placed his queen on the litter bed.

"Thank you," she said with a rasping breath. "You are an honorable man." She smiled up at him before allowing her head to fall back onto the cushioned bed of the litter. Henry could not bring himself to smile back; Jane's frail figure was too dismal a sight. He instead nodded and rose, placing his hands on his hips so that his footman, carrying his garbs, might finish outfitting him. He draped the king's dark green robe across his shoulders and covered it with a thick string of medallions. With a sword placed at his hip and a hat positioned atop his sweating head, Henry's ensemble was complete. All the while, the king gazed down at his weak wife. His heart heavy, he watched her chest rise and fall.

Moments later, when Jane raised her head to look at Henry, he realized their company had fallen silent. He jolted back into action, sending servants back to their positions and instructing the men to prepare themselves. "We are headed to Edward's christening," he began in the strongest voice he was able to muster while great sadness pushed against his broad chest. "Carry Her Highness with the greatest of care towards the chapel."

The men nodded and bowed to the king. Henry waved a hand at their bent figures, and they moved to stand at the ends of the litter. Bending at the knees, they positioned their shoulders underneath the smooth wooden rods extending across the structure. "Slowly rise," a man in the rear commanded. The men's steady knees extended, with Jane left swaying on her litter.

"My love," she whispered, her limp wrist lying across the rail of the bed that hovered inches over the ground. "Please do walk beside me."

Henry stepped forward. He took Jane's hand in his, squeezed it, and placed it over Jane's stomach. Jane smiled a faltering grin up at Henry.

The king looked away, his eyes becoming wet. "Let us move onwards," he said, and the company began to move across the courtyard.

When they approached the chapel, their pace slowed as the men wove their way along the outdoor corridors through the back of the palace. Through arches and windows, light and shadows passed over the gathering. The sunlight brushed over Jane's face after a few steps of darkness. She opened her eyes and glanced over at the gardens beyond. Henry looked down at his queen, studying her complexion. The warm light served to make her white skin seem a dull grey. With clouded eyes, Jane looked over the inviting gardens just beyond the exterior of the corridor. She sighed in disappointment and shivered, turning away from the gardens she knew her feeble legs would not allow her to roam.

"Stop, sirrah," Henry shouted to the leading man, and in a rippling motion, the procession came to a stop. With a slight bump, Jane's litter was placed on the ground.

"Is something the matter, Your Majesty?" asked one of the carriers between strained breaths.

"I require a moment." Henry tapped one of the young ladies in the procession on the shoulder, signaling her to follow him. He ducked under a stone archway into the chapel court gardens, and she followed. The flowers within were withered, their stems hunched over and their petals curled into themselves. Henry scanned the gardens, searching. He whispered to the young lady by his side, who nodded eagerly and jogged off to the far side of the gardens.

"Has something gone wrong?" Jane inquired, trying to push herself upwards for a better look. Her maid rushed forward and put a hand on her shoulder, lowering her back onto the pillows.

"King Henry seems to have disappeared into the gardens."

"For what purpose? The ceremonies must begin soon if they are to be completed in a punctual manner."

"I do not know, My Queen. I could not say."

Jane relaxed in relief when Henry returned. He stepped through the archway with his robe billowed out behind him. It settled, and Jane saw the object in Henry's closed hands: a bundle of flowers. He stepped closer and dropped to one knee, eye-level with Jane. "My beautiful wife, it occurred to me, as I saw the rings of flowers out in the chapel gardens, that you never did truly become my queen." Henry unfolded his hands, revealing long stems of drooping goldenrods and a single, faded red poppy had been twisted together to form a ragged circle. Henry placed the band of wilted fall flowers atop Jane's head. "I am no archbishop, but I do hope that you might accept this crown as a temporary means of coronation."

Jane let out a gentle laugh. "I am certainly willing."

Henry smiled at his wife, taking her hand and planting a soft kiss on its cold surface.

"Pardon me, Your Majesty," said the head of the party. "The chapel music does begin to sound, and we surely must move on if we wish to complete the necessary ceremonies."

"Then we shall. Young Edward awaits us all." Henry smiled down at his wife. She smiled in return. Her weak grin turned to a grimace when her litter was hoisted into the air.

Henry stood back and allowed the procession to move forward. With rising frustration and anger, he watched the grand group carry his withering wife towards his chapel.

The king looked up at the golden cross balanced above the archway of the chapel doors. From here, he had fled to dispose of his first queen. He had looked to its blue painted ceiling and cursed the life of his devious second wife, a devilish woman who still haunted his sleep. He now waited outside the chapel for the death of his most beloved third wife. Henry clamped his fists closed and raised his gaze higher, looking beyond the cross. "God, how do you inflict this great pain on me?" he called out. "What have I done to deserve this unjust reward?" He looked away from the cross and readjusted the robe about his shoulders. "I am a king!" Henry said, voice growing louder. "How dare you do this to me?" He tore his hat from his head, ran his hands through his hair, and stomped his foot. "I have suffered enough..." His voice trailed off. Henry heard the chiming of the church's grand organ and straightened his back. With a large, hot hand, he swiped at his red eyes. He drew in a deep breath and walked into the chapel with his head held level, eyes soberly fixed ahead.

Divorced

BEFORE ANNE IS ANNULLED

"I cannot possibly stay married to that Flanders mare any longer, let alone conceive a child with the woman!" Over the roar of the palace's stone stoves, Anne heard the loud boom of Henry's voice. His hard footsteps clattered across the floors and grew louder and louder as he moved through the hall.

"But Your Majesty, the lady does offer some means of alliance for – "

"Oh, for Heaven's sake," Henry interrupted. Anne cringed when the door to the kitchen shook, a heavy body leaning against it for support. "The King of France and the Roman Emperor have returned to their classic state of animosity, and an alliance is of no use to England any longer. I have no desire to become involved in their tension. England is not willing for war. My marriage to Anne of Cleves thus benefits me in no manner, and I do implore that you seek her out and request that our marriage is annulled within the day so that I might pursue a true interest in the near future." With that, Henry shoved open the wooden door and left a stunned advisor, mouth agape, under the archway.

"Great King, I must insist that we continue this discussion, perhaps at a later time when your thoughts are more gathered," the advisor said. In response, the king slammed the wooden door shut. The man jumped back just in time to avoid a flattened face.

Anne watched the king lean his head against the closed door and let out a frustrated breath. Henry was outfitted in his typical attire, an all black ensemble. A thick cloak lay across his back, the black material accented only by a jewel chain that rested across his shoulders and chest. The monarch turned to face the hot kitchen behind him. "A seat," he commanded, and a baker dropped his dough to pull out a stool for the king. Henry plopped down onto the stool and groaned, pushing his bad leg out in front of him. He nodded at the man who scurried back to his station, taking up his dough and reworking it into an oval shape.

"My King, a simple please tacked on to one's request never hurt a royal man," Anne said in a patient voice.

"Why, by what standard do you see yourself fit to instruct a man such as myself — " Henry began, cutting off as he caught sight of Anne from across the room. His tense shoulders loosened, and he looked away from her accusatory gaze, eyes dropping to the breadbaskets about her feet. He glanced back up and continued. "A king does not need to lower his level by extending any means of politeness to his subjects, Anne. It is unnecessary and so very common."

"Perhaps so," Anne responded. "You may very well be correct, Your Majesty." She stepped forward and made her way through the cooks and servants in the kitchen to where Henry was seated. "However, one is received with more admiration when he can not only speak with respect to those of his status, but even with those he and society deem below him."

"Anne, I did not come to this place to receive a lecture from an ignoble such as yourself," Henry retorted. "Cease this mothering or I must rule for your absence."

Anne leaned back against the wooden table behind her. "For what reason might Your Highness have ventured to this servant's kitchen, then?" Anne crossed her arms under her chest and looked at Henry with a smug smile. It was well known that the king did not take pleasure in this woman's appearance, but the German woman was not of meager looks. Her eyes and mouth were soft, her skin fair, and her hair smooth. Though flat chested, her figure was well flattered in a French styled dress that cinched inwards at her uppermost waist. The deep orange dress ballooned about her shoulders and fell down around her slender wrists.

Henry narrowed his eyes. "It has been quite an eventful day, and I simply needed a place of rest where the other courtiers might not impose upon my time." He smiled back at Anne with brash confidence.

"I am sure," she responded. Anne uncrossed her arms. "Resorting to your privy chambers would never accomplish such a desire. Your appearance here is most assuredly not motivated by a desire or attempt to avoid me." Anne smirked.

"What a ridiculous notion!" Henry countered. "Were I trying to avoid my own queen, I would not take refuge in a servant's kitchen." Anne raised a thin eyebrow. "Regardless, I was not trying to do as such. What, might I ask, are *you* doing in this kitchen?"

Without a word, Anne lifted a hand and pointed across the room. Henry followed her gesture to see a damp cloth draped across a misshapen lump on one of the tables near the walls of the kitchen's oven. Sensing his confusion, Anne clarified. "My ladies and I are preparing some loaves to distribute throughout town tomorrow morning."

"Why ever would you do that? There are plenty of bakeries in the kingdom for suitable men and women to purchase their goods."

Henry crinkled his nose in disgust.

"Have you ever considered that some are unable to do so?" Anne chided. "Many are unable to scrape together the expense for a simple helping of corn, let alone a fresh loaf of bread. There are poor on the streets, and they deserve full stomachs as much as the next." Anne noticed her voice rising in volume, and took a deep breath through her nose before continuing. "So," she said, sighing. "I, along with my ladies, thought it a kind idea to prepare as much bread as possible – baskets full of it – to parade into the town tomorrow."

Henry scowled at Anne's cheery smile. "Why must you use my palace's resources to do so?"

"Why," Anne began, taken aback. "Is it not a queen's job to care and show compassion to her people? From when I was but a young child, I began to learn how to bake. My mother taught me how to fill a bowl with newly harvested yeast, adding in water and but a sprinkle of sugar to the mix. She showed me how to add this mixture to heaps of flour – " Anne lifted her hands, displaying the white powder dusted across her palms. " – and stir the two together. Having learned all these skills, for what purpose would I conceal them from others? As queen, it seems only fair to share my good fortune with those people over whom I preside."

"At the cost of your own courts?" Henry asked, irritated. "You know so very little about the life of royalty, Anne."

"The life of royalty appears to be one of silly trivialities and snobbishness." Anne huffed and wiped her hands across the skirts of her dress. "It does not suit me," she proclaimed. "These dresses are far too extravagant. I cannot stand to hold my head so high and my back so straight, to compose myself in a manner so regal. I am not educated in the ways of my ladies. Even they see that this lifestyle is not fit for me. While I wait here by the fire for my dough to rise, they scurry off to their chambers to wash the yeast from beneath their fingernails and change their dresses so not to be seen in any clothes covered in grime. The flour upon *my* hands and chest could not bother me less." Anne sat down on a stool and looked over to Henry. "I am not fit for the reign of a queen."

"Yes, well, you made that much quite clear upon your entrance to these courts," Henry said. "If I do recall, your clavichord playing was an utter disgrace to behold."

"I will keenly admit that it was," Anne retorted. "But only if you admit how dreadful and rude you were to me upon hearing my playing."

***

Anne sat at a clavichord, fingers clunking across the tan keys of the spindly instrument before her. "Stop," an instructor said patiently, leaning over Anne. Her fingers froze in place, and the teacher took up her left ring finger and moved it down a key. "The note to be played is a C, my dear, not a D." Anne nodded and began the piece over, pressing out each note with deliberate jabs. Again, her fingers faltered. Sour notes sounded throughout the music hall. "Wrong again."

"I am so sorry," Anne said, looking up at the woman and dropping her hands from the keys. "This is only my second attempt at recreating such intricate music myself."

"Not to worry, My Lady. Let us begin again."

Anne nodded and turned back to the clavichord. She placed her fingertips on the keys and began to play. The door flew open and the king, dressed in his regular black attire, strode in.

"What is that horrendous sound?" he roared. Anne placed her hands in her lap.

"Never before in my life have my ears been so tortured by such a despicable noise," the king continued with a grimace. "Have you no musical education, madam?"

"It was not the way I was raised," Anne responded, staring straight.

"Majesty, if I might vouch on behalf of the good lady," the instructor chimed in. "She has made some progress since her first lesson just days ago. She rarely even trips over the opening lines of this new lullaby."

"But it is a child's song," Henry exclaimed. The king dropped his black cloak from his shoulders and heaved it into the hands of the music instructor. Moving to the bench where Anne sat, Henry nudged the new queen over and sat down. Taking the weight off of his right leg, he let out a hiss of relief. "Even the simplest of players should be able to master its tune." Henry chuckled to himself. "I have heard a courtier's son string together the notes with more elegance than you have."

Anne turned to meet Henry's eyes with a steady glare. "I have not been raised in such a musical court as this. I can not be blamed for my inadequacy in this area, Your Majesty."

"Oh," Henry huffed. "You are but three days in this court, Madam. You have little right to talk to me in such a stubborn manner, you… you, you Flanders mare!" Anne looked away, hiding her watering eyes from the king. "This playing is appalling in all senses," Henry affirmed. "It is as if you were raised in a mere pig's sty. This level of skill is unsatisfactory for the elegant and educated position of a queen and my own wife."

Anne turned back to the king and wiped the tears from her cheeks. "My King, I apologize that my playing has hurt you so much." Anne swept herself off the edge of her seat and stood beside the clavichord. "I shall continue working to improve my skills." The new queen paused before adding, "You may consider changing how you brand another's character based on one's few inefficiencies." She fumbled into a curtsy and turned to leave, holding her heavy skirts up by the tips of her fingers. Anne's instructor handed Henry his cloak, hurried to gather her music in her arms, mumbled an apology to the king, and scrambled away after her queen. *The doors slammed, and Henry was left sitting alone.*

***

"It was not I who was rude." Henry crossed his arms over his chest.

"You compared my complexion to that of a common stable horse!" Anne snapped, the teasing smile dropping from her face. "That is no way to refer to a lady. Your status as king does not justify your poor treatment of others, royal and otherwise."

"Your lack of education is so downright crass – "

"Cease this regard of my lesser education," Anne said. The king let out a low gulp, not used to being interrupted. Anne's confidence waned for a moment, her chin dipping low in an ashamed motion. The king's brow began to tighten. Anne raised her head to once again meet his gaze. "My inability to play the clavichord does not define my character as a whole. Are you still so blind to that as when we first met?"

"I am blind to very little," Henry said, tossing his cloak back over his shoulders. "During my past thirty year reign, pain has been known to me in manners both emotional and physical." Henry gestured to his weak leg. "This cursed injury from years back does cause my leg to ache so thoroughly, and more and more so by each day that comes and goes. Lowly people and grand nations have betrayed me. God, who does supposedly watch over me and my kingdom, has stolen from me child and wife." Henry's demeanor shifted, his expression narrowing and his fists clenching. "To claim that I am blind by any means is a deep offense to me."

Anne sat up straight and crossed her ankles beneath her. She took a deep breath and released it in a slow exhale, watching the king all the while. "I do not doubt that you know suffering," she responded. "There is not a grain of doubt in my mind that a monarch such as yourself has faced times of struggle in his time to

81

rule such a great land." Anne paused. She rose from her stool and took a step towards Henry. Lightly, she placed a hand on his shoulder and looked him in the eye. "However, *My Lord*," she continued with a disdainful chuckle. "These experiences do not negate those of others. Had you ever considered that I left my household, my family, my own land to come dwell in these courts? I gave up a peaceful life of housework and regular marriage to live in this lonely palace where new languages and talents are forced upon me. All the while, I live with a king who chastises my appearance and skulks about with other women." Anne removed her hand from Henry's shoulder and folded her arms over her smock.

"I do not skulk about with other women," Henry said. "A king should not frolic about while he is committed to another."

"A king *also* should not lie." The harsh edge returned to Anne's voice. "Do not pretend that the words I speak are not the truth. Do not pretend to be ignorant to the fact that I have seen that young Kathryn waltz about in the same gowns that you presented to me in my own closet."

Henry grumbled, but no honest response came to his mind. Anne nodded, turned from the king, and made her way around the large center table to her dough. She peeled back the cloth, dumping it into a basket filled with other yeasty towels. The risen dough lay before her. Anne took it into her hands and folded the wet sides together, tucking them inside the dough. Then, eyeing it, Anne divided it into two rounds. She glanced to Henry, who was observing each of her motions. Anne returned her attention to the project before her. She took both rounds and molded them into loaves with slow, steady kneading.

Leaving the dough on the table, Anne whisked about the kitchen, taking butter from one cook, baskets from one, and clean cloths from another. Back at the table, she rubbed the soft butter across the top of her dough. It slid across the surface and down the sides. Henry grimaced, as Anne's rough hands became grubbier, butter glistening across her fingers. Anne scraped the remaining dough from her hands onto the tabletop, then took two cloths and draped one across each loaf.

"Good sir," she called to a cook across the kitchen. "Will the oven shelves be warmed once the bread has risen?"

"Yes, Queen Anne," he called in response. He nodded his head in a swift and gallant gesture.

"Many thanks."

The man's face lit up and he nodded. "Whatever might help, My Lady," he responded and returned to his business.

Anne turned back to face Henry. "As you might note, manners and politeness do no harm to me, and concurrently warm the heart of another." Henry grumbled in response, but found no retort for the woman. After a moment's pause, she leaned against the center table and directed her gaze at the king. "You are welcome to retreat to this kitchen," Anne said, breaking the silence between the two. "But if you truly hope to avoid me, you may wish to leave, My King." Henry did not respond. "The heat does not bode well with your aching leg, I am sure," she added in an attempt to provoke the king's departure.

He continued to stare at Anne.

Anne stared back, not allowing herself to look away from the man's heavy gaze.

Minutes passed. The faint sounds of the kitchen workers bustling about was the only noise left drifting between the two. They watched one another with understanding eyes, the tense feeling of the dropped conversation sinking around them.

Henry broke first. "I shall be taking my fifth wife in sixteen days, Anne."

"I supposed that were the case," Anne responded, attempting a nonchalant shrug. "I shall be gone from this home by the time sixteen days has passed then, Your Majesty."

"I hope this should be the case," Henry said. Anne frowned, but remained silent. "You are welcome to move to Hever Castle upon your dismissal, if such be your wish. Here, you might make silly use of the land's resources and bake bread to your heart's desire."

Anne scoffed. "I shall be sure to do so."

Henry nodded. "You were…" he started, voice trailing off as any form of compliment escaped his mind.

"Unrefined? Gauche? Not fit to be a queen?" Anne tilted her head. "Take your pick. I am aware of these facts, and they bother me little. It is with a weighty heart that I shall leave this kingdom, for its people are so kind." Anne glanced about the kitchen. "But please enjoy your time with your new wife, Great King." Anne wiped off the front of her dress and curtsied for Henry.

The king, confused emotions causing his head to throb, nodded in return. He stood and gave a slight bow. "I… I do appreciate you taking your time to take the position of my wife."

"I willingly pass it on to your Kathryn."

"Yes," Henry said, unable to respond otherwise.

Anne forced a small smile. "I must attend to my loaves now," she said, gesturing to the thick dough that had begun to rise on the table behind her. "There are many more to yet be prepared."

"I ought to be elsewhere," Henry countered. He once again nodded to his wife and began to leave. Through each step that he lumbered towards the door, the pain in his injured leg began to increase.

"If you happen to come across my ladies," Anne called as the king left. "Please do send them my way." Henry continued to stride away. "And Henry?" Anne added. His hot, heavy footsteps ceased. Henry swiveled halfway to face Anne once more.

"Do take care with these other women," Anne said. "There is far more at stake than your own frivolous feelings."

Henry clenched his fists by his side and turned to walk away. He shoved open the kitchen door, not bothering to close it gently. Anne startled at the slam of the door. Her shoulders dropped in disappointment at the king's dismissal of her warning words.

Beheaded

FLAWED PEARLS

Kathryn, waltzing away from the clock tower of Hampton Court, tugged loose the pearls that had tightened around her neck so that she might breathe better. With her fur shawl bunched up in her arms, Kathryn slid her rings back onto her fingers. Unfurling her shawl, she noticed the top of her dress was still askew. She rushed to adjust it before draping her shawl between her elbows and about her back.

"Lady Kathryn!" cried a voice from afar. Wary, Kathryn paused and looked about. At center court, a young lady waved at the queen. Two others nodded at Kathryn from behind the eager woman.

Letting out a sigh of relief, Kathryn raised her hand in greeting and smiled. "Joan, dearest," she called. The waving woman made her way to Kathryn, leaving behind the pair of chattering gossips. As she walked towards Kathryn, the trail of her bright dress skimmed across the cobblestones beneath her sprightly feet. Kathryn could not help but to smile at Joan's cheerful step, her smile widening as the girls neared one another.

Joan picked up her skirts and curtsied to Kathryn before popping back up and giggling. "The whole concept of curtsying to you, my closest friend, holds much humor to me, *Queen* Kathryn," she said.

"Oh," the young queen responded in amusement. "Am I not worthy of being bowed to, Joan?" She straightened her shoulders and mockingly folded her fingers together in front of her midriff. "That is a bold implication to direct towards a queen. I could have you beheaded for even mentioning such a notion!"

Joan laughed. "The thought would barely cross your mind, my Kathryn. Without me, with whom might you confide your deepest secrets?" Joan raised an eyebrow and glanced back as the women in the distance leaned over, whispering to one another. "Not your royal ladies who do wait so patiently to take your crown from you when your life here does end."

"I am but a young woman, aged only nineteen years – far less, even, than yourself. My death resides far in the future." Kathryn shrugged. "My age is far too new for these gossiping ladies to ever have the chance to even glance upon my throne." Kathryn's voice raised, then faded off into light laughter. "The idea is ridiculous."

"For once, I believe you are right," Joan said in return. With her eye on the queen's ladies in waiting, Joan leaned to Kathryn and lowered her voice. "Now, be true. Where did Her Highness disappear to this afternoon, when she had lessons to attend?"

Looking up at Joan, Kathryn put on an innocent smile. "I was simply about the yards with my visiting family." Joan scoffed. "I had to show them around the courts, for they have never come to this place before," Kathryn insisted, her expression mischievous all the while.

"If such is the case, where are these members? I see no family by your side." Joan crossed her arms and looked beyond Kathryn's shoulder, pretending to search for anyone who might be behind her in the distance.

Kathryn stepped to the side to block Joan's view. "Emergency called them back home. They were sent off in the swiftest of carriages but minutes ago."

"So, if I perchance stroll to the stables at this near dinner hour, I will find it missing two carriage horses?" Joan sidestepped around Kathryn and began striding away from center court, a hop in her step. Kathryn ran after her, taking hold of her wrist and twirling her around.

"Perhaps they weren't sent off in a carriage," she said, swift to amend her story. "Perhaps they were... they decided to walk back to the village for the evening." Kathryn crossed her arms.

"You will need a far more convincing story than that to explain your absence from your lessons to the king."

"Why, I shall tell him that I was occupied with – "

"Hush," Joan interrupted. She widened her eyes and subtly nodded to something behind Kathryn. "Your ladies do approach."

Kathryn pursed her lips and turned around. The two women were indeed approaching, their arms linked together as they stepped towards Kathryn and Joan. The lady on the left curtsied and asked in a timid tone, "My Queen, are you quite ready for dinner? The hour approaches, and we do see gentlemen of this court making their ways towards the hall for dining."

"I..." Kathryn began, looking to Joan.

Her friend stepped forward, placing a hand on Kathryn's upper arm and directing her soft gaze at the ladies. "Lady Kathryn is hungry as well, but must visit her privy chambers to adjust her hair and outfitting after such a long day of lessons and visitors." Joan paused before adding, "But please, you must be beyond famished. Make your way to the hall and feast. We will be but a quarter of an hour away."

"Do be swift," the second woman interjected. "You know the

king's temper does not hold long for his women, particularly not when urged on by an empty stomach." She raised an eyebrow at Kathryn and turned away.

Kathryn nodded and smiled, keeping silent as the two ladies strolled away towards the hall beside the court's grand kitchens. Joan placed a hand on Kathryn's waist and began to guide her towards the staircase leading to the palace's apartments. Once they had rounded the corner, they ducked into the stairwell, concealed within the shadows of the towering walls and looming steps.

"You *must* be more careful," Joan instructed, a light smile no longer playing across her face.

"I *am* careful."

"You have a reputation, Kathryn." The young queen huffed and looked away. Joan gripped Kathryn's chin and turned her slim face back towards her, staring at her with steely eyes. "Before we were even acquainted, rumors did float about the royal lines and towns that you were a girl of... unique intrigue and prowess. Though you have aged and your neck carries the pearls and pendants of Henry, you must remain aware. Your ladies are at all times by your side, and when they are not, they must have reason for your disappearance."

"And I always give them such reason," Kathryn retorted.

"Not good reason," Joan countered. "If you are to lie, it must become like an art to you. You cannot roam about the courts and chambers with whatever man may catch your eye, as you used to. If you insist on this type of trickery – which, if I might take leeway to comment on it myself, is far too risky a territory to explore with a marriage to a king of such reputation as Henry – you must be more careful."

"That I am." Kathryn met Joan's firm gaze. "The king suspects nothing. Even if he were to find some fault in my stories, I am far more youthful than his other wives. He treats me more like a beloved daughter than a wife. He would give everything to attend to my whims." Joan opened her mouth to respond, but was cut off as Kathryn continued. "My fate cannot be predicted by that of his other wives. Things have changed, and circumstances are different."

"Yet," Joan pointed out. "He is the same man, with the same temperament. He beheaded one of your own cousins. Do not feel so certain he is beyond appointing the same destiny to you."

"The king is infatuated with me." Kathryn again looked away, glancing around the corner of the stairwell at the darkening sky. "It is *not* a concern of mine."

Joan let her hands drop to her sides. "Maybe it ought to be," she chided. Kathryn rolled her eyes and attempted to respond. "No," Joan continued. "I shall hear nothing more on the matter. Let us retreat to the dining hall so that you might avoid further reason for suspicion, my dear friend."

Kathryn remained silent, pulling her lips into a thin, tight line. She looped her arm through Joan's, and the two hurried towards the warm hall where dinner was being spread across the tables. The two separated as they entered the long hall, Kathryn stepping through the cream arch first.

"My Queen," a voice boomed from the end of the room. Kathryn arched her neck and caught the eye of Henry, seated at his private table. "Join me, my fair wife." Kathryn raised a hand in greeting. Heads swiveled to the entrance of the room, eyes fixed on her. She put on a smile and made her way down the center aisle between long stretches of polished tables. The occasional man rose to greet Kathryn, and she daintily offered her hand to each for a kiss. Joan followed in a similar manner, dropping off to sit with a table of Kathryn's whispering ladies.

A minute later, Kathryn stood before Henry. The redness of his face deepened as she dipped into a low curtsy before him. "Your Highness," she said. He nodded his head in approval. She rose and walked around to the seat beside him, a cushioned red throne decorated in golden fringe. Kathryn placed a hand on Henry's broad shoulder and beamed a bright smile at him before sitting down in her seat, hands folded across her lap. A servant walked forward to remove her fur shawl so that Kathryn could allow her arms to relax.

Taking up a thick piece of sliced beef from his plate, Henry shouted across the room, "Queen Kathryn has arrived. I welcome her, and you wonderful courtiers and secretaries, to dine with us on this evening." Henry stuffed his beef into his mouth and looked to Kathryn expectantly. She glanced down and plucked a small piece of fish off her plate with her fingers. As soon as she began to chew, the other members of the court presiding at the dinner sat down and began to fill their plates with food. Kathryn smiled in satisfaction.

"How was your day, My King?" she asked, batting her eyelashes at Henry as she chewed through a piece of salted herring.

"Dull while you were not around," he responded. "How did your lessons fare?"

"Quite well, I do say," she said, looking away from the king. She picked up a grape from her plate and popped it into her mouth. "My instructor says my Latin has progressed immensely."

"Incredible," the king praised. "An entire day spent on Latin is a feat to be proud of. You are a young wife of many talents."

"Well…" Kathryn said, twisting in her seat to look at Henry. "I did not spend the *entirety* of my day on lessons." Henry finished off his portion of beef and looked to Kathryn in confusion. Kathryn remembered Joan's warning and sat up straight, careful not to clear her throat and appear nervous. "My mother and uncle, Duke of Norfolk, as you may recall, came from London to call upon me earlier this day. I did show them round the courts for the afternoon before they were rushed off in all urgency to see my father."

"Oh!" Henry exclaimed, eyes wide. "You did not tell me that your family visited today. Why did you keep this visitation from me?"

"Why, I thought you would be too busy for such matters, love." Kathryn spoke with confidence and maintained eye contact with her husband.

"I am a man of many duties, but I am always able to make time for the family of my own dear wife."

"My King," Kathryn continued, searching for excuses. "I also took into account the condition of your leg. It does need as much rest as might be possible for a man as magnificent and busy as yourself."

Henry paused. "I reason you are not wrong." He turned back to his plate, this time eating a large piece of duck. "Do consult me the next time such a visit occurs, Kathryn," he said stiffly.

Kathryn nodded and ate on in silence, letting her gaze wander about the room. Joan caught her eye and tilted her head in question. Kathryn smiled and gave a slight nod before continuing to sweep the room. Just as she returned to her meal, a man strode inside, thumbs tucked into his belt as he sauntered towards an empty seat. A sly smile crept onto Kathryn's face, and she arched her neck, narrowing her eyes, waiting for the man to glance at her. He soon looked up and winked at the queen, gesturing with one finger for Kathryn to join him. Kathryn raised her eyebrows in response and covered her mouth to contain a girlish giggle. She turned to Henry, tapping his arm for his attention. "My King, I am being summoned by your dear courtier, Culpepper. Might I leave your side to discuss with him for a brief time? He has joined me in my lessons as of late, and has been so devoted in attempting to explain the politics of our day to me." Kathryn leaned towards Henry, looking up at him with soft eyes. "There are but a few more questions I wish to impose upon his mind."

"I suppose you might…" Henry glanced over to where Thomas Culpepper sat, making conversation with young women and court members. "Culpepper has proven himself a wise, honest man." Henry looked back to his half-empty plate. "You may take your leave."

"Oh, thank you, my gracious husband." Kathryn stood and leaned to kiss the top of the king's head before she lifted her skirts from the floor and made her way down the steps from the royal dais. Henry watched her prance away, then sit down on the bench beside Thomas. From across the room, Joan shot a warning glance to Kathryn. The young queen was too engulfed in playing with Thomas's coat buttons to heed the harsh look from her friend.

"More food," Henry barked to a servant, all the while watching Kathryn. A servant took his plate and piled it up with a plentiful amount of mutton and fruit. Henry waved his hand and the man retreated. As the king ate, shoving mutton into his mouth, his eyes remained fixed on Kathryn. She leaned forward and placed her hand on Thomas's forearm. Henry watched in annoyance as his queen's head fell back in laughter, her hair falling back from her pretty face. She raised her head once again. Her eyes were soft, with a look not unlike the one she had just lent to Henry.

"Your Majesty," a voice called from behind the king, causing him to spook and swivel around. Behind him stood Archbishop Cranmer, Henry's advisor and personal friend. He held two items against his chest, a worn Bible and collection of tattered paper. They pressed his pointed white beard against his clothing. His black and white robes were loose around his stomach, draping down to his thin ankles. He stepped closer to the king. "Your Majesty, I must speak with you immediately."

"Cranmer. You are the exact man I had hoped to encounter," Henry said. The king turned back around, gesturing for Cranmer to join him.

Confused, the advisor moved forward to stand beside the king. "Why might that be, Your Majesty?" Cranmer asked.

Henry lifted a finger and pointed across the room to Kathryn. "You know the face of my wife. I am correct in this assumption?"

"Why, yes, I have met her on many – "

"Yes, of course," Henry interrupted. He reached out, finger still pointing across the room. Cranmer looked to where he pointed, spotting Kathryn seated among the courtiers. "You see her there?"

"That I do, Highness." Cranmer paused. "Might I be so bold as to ask why she dines out there, rather than by your gracious side?"

Henry, his brow furrowed, looked to Cranmer. "I ask myself that, as well." Henry turned back to watch Kathryn, just as she leaned toward Thomas and brushed her shoulder against his. "Look! There."

Cranmer's eyes narrowed. "What am I looking at, My Good King?"

"Do her movements not seem rather forward to you? The way she leans towards the man in orange with a hand at his elbow? It seems ever so strange to me." Henry dropped his hand to the table.

Cranmer took a step backwards and straightened. "Actually, My King, that matter does relate to the issue I came here to present."

Henry turned to face the Archbishop. "What issue might that be?"

"The problem pertains to your queen, Kathryn," Cranmer began, looking to Henry for permission to continue on this sensitive subject. The king waved an anxious hand and Cranmer continued. "It is not uncommon knowledge that prior to your betrothal to Miss Howard, the lady did maintain a rather scandalous reputation. It was often thought that she was marginally... promiscuous in her dealings with other men. When she came to this court, we became aware of a tendency – perhaps just rumors, at the time – for Kathryn to engage in inappropriate conversation and actions with members of this court. The matter really is quite dreadful, and – "

"Good God, Cranmer. Do get to the point," Henry cut in.

"Yes, well…" Cranmer said, clutching his Bible and papers against his chest. "There is now quite definitive reason to believe that Kathryn has been…" He trailed off and looked up at the towering ceilings. Cranmer let out a slow breath. His voice dropped to a hush. "Kathryn has known another man during her marriage to you, Highness."

Henry paused. "I cannot…" His eyes narrowed. "My illness must be getting to me. I am certain I have misheard you. Might you repeat that?"

Cranmer placed his Bible down and shuffled through his papers, to the fourth piece of parchment. "Members of your advisory court, myself included, have kept note of Kathryn's whereabouts and handlings." Cranmer handed the paper to Henry. "We have two new sources – gentle and distraught ladies from the court – who do claim that Kathryn was untruthful about her whereabouts today. We followed these claims and found they were correct. This, in addition to a few other moves by the queen, led us to declare her adulterous behavior."

Henry stared at his hands. "That's preposterous. There is no man for whom Kathryn would leave my side."

"This was our presumption as well, My King." Cranmer began flipping through his papers once again. "We thus deemed it necessary to find a male culprit to present." Cranmer showed Henry a page marked with charts and dates. "A few select gentlemen fell under our suspicion. Upon inspection of their recent schedules – as they coincided with Queen Kathryn's – we have determined that she has known Thomas Culpepper."

Henry stood, ignoring the pain that shot through his leg. "Kathryn!" he shouted across the hall, silencing all who sat eating. All eyes turned to the king. They saw his angered face and bowed their heads towards the tables in respect. Kathryn too looked over, removing her hands from Thomas's shoulder. Henry's gaze swiveled to Thomas, who had, to Henry's shock, a hand placed tenderly on the small of Kathryn's back. This hand also pulled away as the pair looked to Henry. "By my side this instant," he commanded, voice bellowing across the grand room and bouncing off the high walls and arches.

Kathryn jumped up from her seat and scurried like a frightened stable mouse to where Henry stood. When Kathryn approached, Henry reached out to grab her upper arm. He held her tight and tugged her forward. "Meet me in the trophy room." Kathryn failed to move. "Now," he said. She stumbled into action, falling out of the king's grip and retreating. Henry looked over the dining hall again. Everyone was still frozen in place. "Resume eating. Do not let such a banquet go to waste," he demanded, causing all to return to their meals. Henry turned to follow Kathryn, whispering to Cranmer before he left. "Do not allow Culpepper to exit. Bring him back here to me." The Archbishop nodded and turned back to the crowd, eyeing the seat from which Culpepper had slunk. The king and Cranmer took off in opposite directions.

Henry retreated behind the wall of the dining hall to where a trembling Kathryn stood, waiting. He limped forward with hard footsteps. Kathryn put up her hands, her stoic face crumbling into a look of fear. "Please, My King, what has afflicted you so?" Henry continued to stride forward as best he could, and Kathryn moved backwards as he did so. "You ought to sit and rest your leg. My love?"

She faltered at the look of anger on Henry's face, giving the king an opportunity to close the gap between them. He moved forward and laid his hand across Kathryn's face with a sharp smack. She dipped to the ground, her hands covering her cheek. "You are not fit to be my queen, nor take the envied position of my wife. Why, you are not even fit to be a proper woman of this court, foolish strumpet." The king backed away from where his young wife lay curled up on the cool floor.

"I am no strumpet," Kathryn bit back, removing her hand from her face so that she could push herself upwards. Her cheek was bright red, matching the shade of the king's heated face.

"You are near enough to the cursed word, little harpy." Kathryn moved to respond but the king continued to scream down at her. "Do not attempt to deny what you have so blatantly done."

"What did I do that is so foul to you, Your Majesty?" Kathryn yelled back tearfully.

Henry let out a rumbling laugh. "Playing innocent, are we, young one? Do you deny that you have known Thomas Culpepper as you did know me on our marital night?"

The accusation lay before her. Kathryn's face turned white as her winter powder. She rose from the ground to face the king. Intertwining her fingers, she lifted her gaze to meet Henry's. "My love, I – "

"Do not call me as such," he interrupted. "Answer my question with the full truth. Have you known Thomas Culpepper while we have been married?"

Kathryn paused. She looked down at her feet. "It is true."

Henry snapped and drew his sword from its sheath. As he did so, Cranmer shoved Culpepper into the room. Henry rushed forward, sword held above his head. "I ought to cut your throat for such obscene adulterous crimes!"

Kathryn dropped to the floor once again, pulling her knees up under her chin and ducking her head. She put her hands up in surrender, pleading, words fast and feverish, with the approaching monarch. "Your Majesty," Archbishop Cranmer called across the room. Henry glanced back for a moment, but continued to move forward, fuming. "Great Henry, you must stop. This is not the place, nor the time. Cease this before blood stains your holy hands and soul."

At this, Henry froze. Sword still clutched in his hand, he turned to face Cranmer. The Archbishop held out his hands in front of him, showing that he intended only peace. Henry saw the cross that balanced on a thread around Cranmer's neck. He let out an unsteady breath and closed his eyes. When he opened them, he turned his gaze to glare at Culpepper. Henry sheathed his sword with a loud scrape. He addressed Cranmer, his eyes throwing daggers at the other man who had soiled his wife. "People of my court wait outside for my address. I must attend to these natural conventions at this time. I shall return to this matter later this evening. Have these two removed from my palace for the time being." Henry straightened his coat. "Be certain to guarantee that the two traitors are unable to speak to each other during their imprisonment."

Thomas opened his mouth and stepped forward, raising a hand to Henry. "Your Highness, I think that request is unreasonable given that – "

"Unreasonable?" Henry asked, hand returning to the hilt of his sword. "Traitor, you do not understand even the slightest implications of the word. You have brought upon me the highest and utmost dishonor. By no right can you speak against me in this moment. Pray, speak another word and see what fate unfolds for you."

Archbishop Cranmer put a hand on Culpepper's shoulder in warning. The courtier stepped back to his place and let his head drop. Henry limped back towards the dining hall. "I shall clean up these matters, Majesty," Cranmer whispered as the king passed by.

"I regret that you must be betrayed in such a way, my friend." He attempted to meet Henry's eye, but the king looked past him with a solid gaze. Cranmer thought he spotted a moment of pain pass over the king's eyes, but the ruler nodded and it disappeared.

Cranmer watched Henry walk out of the room, holding his chest high. When he had rounded the corner, Cranmer took Thomas by the arm. He dragged him to the door and called in two guards from the dining hall. They held Thomas tight while Cranmer crossed the room to where Kathryn lay, weeping. "Rise, woman." She let out a shuddering sob. Cranmer wiped hair back from her face and pushed on her shoulder. "I say, Kathryn, relinquish yourself from this pity and stand up from the floor."

Kathryn wiped a sleeve across her nose and stood. She avoided looking over to Thomas, who stared at her. "Where are we to be held? What is to become of us?" she asked Cranmer.

"That I cannot yet answer." Cranmer crossed the room, a hand on Kathryn's shoulder to lead her to the guards. "Time will reveal the punishment for the crime committed here."

With this, Cranmer retrieved his papers from within his cloak. He handed one to the man nearest him. Upon reading the charge, the men took the two lovers, Thomas by the wrists and Kathryn by the arm, and led them towards the back of the trophy room.

Thomas kept his head high and tried to shake his guard's grip. Kathryn kept her head bowed. With a shaking hand, she reached up to touch her throat. Remembering Joan's warning about Kathryn's cousin, the young queen let out a stifled cry, and tears began to fill her eyes once again. Her hand dropped to the pearls that lay across her chest. Her fingers clutched the necklace as she was escorted from Henry's palace, all hope and confidence gone.

Survived

FOR THE KING

Katherine sat under the shade of the cherry blossom tree, watching Thomas as he paced in front of her, the wind blowing his red beard back in his face. He attempted to flatten it each time, to no avail. His typically dull brown eyes were lit up with an intensity that Katherine had only had the pleasure of seeing a few times. "Thomas, please cease this senseless walking. It will do nothing for the state of our situation."

"No, it will not," Thomas replied, ripping his hat from his head and wringing it in his hands. He continued walking back and forth, feet trampling Katherine's flowers. She was about to scold him for ruining them when he stopped and turned to her. "I have a proposal," Thomas said, gazing down at Katherine. She looked up to him with curiosity.

"Well, speak it then," she insisted, and folded her hands across the skirts of her modest blue dress. Thomas sat down beside her. He placed a hand atop of hers, and she shook it off, turning her head to look at the empty gravel path just outside the stone wall of her property. She turned back to Thomas who nodded, retracting his hand and placing his hat back atop his head, shining with sweat. He knew it was risky enough for him and Katherine to be meeting, let alone be caught touching one another, even if it were just a brush of the fingers.

"Do not marry the king," Thomas said in a hushed voice.

Katherine rolled her eyes, letting her shoulders slump. As her posture weakened, the tight waist of her dress cut into her side, and Katherine grimaced. She straightened again and replied, "I thought I made matters perfectly clear. One cannot refuse the courtship of King Henry."

"Of course. But if you were to disappear, he would have no choice but to – "

"Thomas, do not speak such... such nonsense. In no manner can I evade marrying the king. If I do not take on the role of his wife, he will have me beheaded. I am sure that is not the outcome either of us is hoping for," Katherine scolded, a tint of red coming to her cheeks.

"No, no... that is not desired." Thomas looked off in thought. "But I do not wish you to marry that currish boar." Thomas turned back to Katherine, his gaze holding hers. "You know of what he did to my sister. She gave him a son, all that he had wanted, and he still allowed her to die. In fact, I would not be surprised if he encouraged my dear Jane's death. I refuse to have your life come to the same end."

"I am well aware of the incident, Thomas," Katherine countered. "It is not as if I wish to be wedded to the king. Wives of King Henry have a tendency to fare poorly... My namesake, Catherine of Aragon, was removed from her throne and banished to another palace." Katherine lowered her voice, as it had begun to rise in volume. "And her fate was far more fortunate than others. The lives of three wives have come to unjust ends under the king. I am in constant fear of becoming the fourth in a line of deceased women."

Thomas leaned forward. "The thought of more women – especially you, my love – meeting the same end as my dearest Jane is unbearable. We cannot stand for such rampant tyranny and betrayal from England's own king."

Katherine turned and moved to away from Thomas. His loud voice was attracting the attention of wandering townspeople. A curious little boy with shaggy golden hair and thin eyebrows pulled himself up to sit on Katherine's garden wall. He pulled one of the looser stones out, rolling it around in his sticky palms. As he settled on the wall, his puffy trousers deflated, and his collar bunched up around his neck. He tugged at it. The red and black lining around the edge tore with a faint ripping sound. "Good e'en, miss!" he called and nodded at Katherine. She smiled back and raised a gentle hand in return. The boy's mother turned around, glaring at her son and pulling him down from the wall. He tumbled down, tripping to his feet and crossing his chubby arms in annoyance.

"My apologies, Miss Parr," called the woman, who noticed her sitting on the grass beside Thomas Seymour. She curtsied to Katherine. Thomas was gazing at Katherine, and only looked away when the villager continued speaking. "And good evening to you, Baron Seymour," she said. She curtsied again.. She looked back and forth between Katherine and Thomas. "Fare both thee well." The woman took her child's hand and gathered up her basket before rushing down the street towards her house.

"Brilliant. Word that we were having a private meeting, in the shade of the trees and the late evening sun no less, will spread by dawn." Katherine rose and brushed the grass from her skirt. "I think it best that you depart, Thomas."

He scrambled to stand up, taking his hat off in order to bow to Katherine. "But what of our engagement?" he whispered.

"There is still time to find a solution," Katherine said. Her voice was low, and smiled uneasily at Thomas. Katherine offered her hand to the man. He took it and pressed his lips to it. "I may have a plan," she said, dipping into a curtsy. She took his arm and led him to the gate at the front of her garden. "I shall convey it to you tomorrow evening, for I still have but a few days prior to my departure for Hampton Court Palace." She opened her gate and gestured for him to exit. "Return then."

"But Katherine," Thomas said. "What do you intend, my love?" He gripped her shoulder and spun her around to face him.

"Hush, Thomas," she admonished. In an anxious voice, she said, "Trust me. I may have a way to get us out of our trap."

***

"Lady Katherine, there really is no need for you to stay here with the cooks. I assure you they will prepare the meal to perfection," the handmaid said, dabbing at Katherine's head with a cool towel. She reached up to sweep away the veil that had come untucked from Katherine's cap. It did little to relieve the heat that came in waves from the stove fires. Katherine was fitted in a beautiful gown, similar to the ones she had grown accustomed to over the last four years as queen. The gown was of French design, with trumpeted sleeves and turned back cuffs lined with fur. The rest of her dress, not including the large farthingale and layers of hot skirt, was made of black velvet. It was plain, with only a few golden threads running up the sides in an intricate pattern that pleased her, but not the dressmaker. However, the man had trimmed her square collar with pearls and had given her a cap laced with the same pearls to make the outfit, as he put it, seem more "royal." In truth, the gown was one of Katherine's simpler ones these days, but that did not mean that the heat from the busy stone stove would not make her cheeks flush red as she sat in the castle's overcrowded kitchen.

"I have no doubt the meal will be delicious, Cicely. The cook's meals are always as such," Katherine responded. She swiped a gloved hand across the back of her sweaty neck. "But I was so hoping to convince the cooks to bake some plum pudding."

"Why, Lady Katherine, this late in the preparations?" Cicely's eyes widened, and she glanced around at the rushing men and women. "The king has called in extra cooks and maids from the nearby towns to work on constructing this brilliant feast. Hundreds of guests will be in attendance for the upcoming celebration. There is hardly time to prepare enough pudding for – "

"No, no, Cicely. Do not fret," Katherine interrupted, smiling at her worried maid. "I simply want to make a small portion for His Majesty, so – "

"Long live King Henry," Cicely murmured to herself. She drew a cross on her chest before urging Katherine to continue.

Katherine nodded in return, mimicking the cross on her own chest. "The doctors say his health has improved as of late, and I therefore believe he deserves a personal celebratory dessert."

"That is wonderful news," Cicely said. "You are such a generous queen, My Lady. I shall let the cooks know." Cicely scurried away to one of the perspiring women, the head of the kitchen, who was stirring a large pot. She whispered in her ear, and the woman looked up to Katherine with a smile and nodded.

Katherine raised herself from her seat in the corner. The room froze. The women ceased their stirring, the men stopped with hands full of meat, and the youths playing in the corner hushed each other to stare at Katherine as she walked into the center of the kitchen.

"Queen Katherine," one woman said, dipping into a curtsy as Katherine approached her. "Please, do not strain yourself. I shall prepare a puddin' for His Majesty. You need not watch so closely among us mere maids." She pulled off her hat and fiddled with it in her hands before curtsying yet again.

"I wish to help," Katherine said. She adjusted her sleeves so the fur along the cuffs would not brush against her hands.

The cook looked shocked. "M-My Lady, that is not necessary. I swear to you that these cooks are the best in the king's lands."

"I do not doubt that. Still, I wish to be of some assistance. I baked for all my family before I became queen, and I make an admirable pudding."

The cook paused before ducking into another bow. "As you wish, Your Highness. You shall work alongside me, and we shall make the beloved king a puddin'." The cook brushed aside some flour from the table in the center of the kitchen. She slammed a large bowl down onto the surface. The other workers took that as a signal to continue their preparations. "I shall get you an apron, as to not stain your dress," the cook said, whirling around and snatching another woman's apron. She handed it to Cicely, who tied it around Katherine's waist. Katherine pulled off her gloves and pearls and handed them to Cicely for safekeeping. She watched as the cook dumped in the ingredients and began to stir everything together. A sloppy brown mixture soon began to form. The cook eyed Katherine and asked, "Would you like to stir, My Lady?"

"Oh, please," Katherine exclaimed, reaching for the spoon. She dragged it through the thick mixture.

"I will run across the courts to get the fruit, chocolate, and brandy," the cook said, and rushed out of the room.

Katherine saw her opportunity. Cicely was standing in the corner of the room, fiddling with the beads the queen had given her to watch; the cook would be gone for a few minutes while in search of fruit and wine; the others were far too stressed and engrossed in their work to notice the queen's actions. Katherine reached down her front, pulling out a brass bottle from where it lay against her chest. She tugged out its cork, tipping it and allowing three drops to spill over into the mixture. She folded the brown slush of pudding over the moist patch and mixed the liquid in. She tucked the bottle back down her bodice, nervous anticipation running through her. She ignored the feeling and finished stirring the pudding, smiling at the cook when she returned to add the remaining ingredients into the bowl.

***

Later that evening, after the celebration, Katherine led Cicely to the king's chambers, keeping a close eye on the silver tray that she carried. The pudding and a tall, gold-rimmed goblet of wine were balanced on the tray. The pair rounded the column at the end of the corridor, where there were two doors with a guard standing out front.

"I am here to visit the king and to bring him this delicacy," Katherine said, gesturing to the dessert Cicely was holding. The guard bowed in return and banged his staff against the floor once.

"I apologize, Your Highness, but the king is supposed to be resting at this time, as the night's ceremonies have taken a toll on his health." Katherine pouted and the guard continued. "This is on order of his personal physician."

"Oh, why, I have just been to see his physician," Katherine retorted. Cicely swiveled her head to look at Katherine. The queen ignored her confused gaze. "The man has seen signs of improvement in the king. I bring him this dish in congratulations."

The guard looked to the tray and back to Katherine. "I suppose it might be permitted in such an instance. But the royal assayer of the court must taste the pudding before I can permit it to Great King Henry this evening." The man stared straight ahead as he spoke.

"I understand. It is procedure. Please continue," Katherine said with a calm expression, though her hands shook. The guard called for a messenger, who jogged off to find the assayer. They returned within minutes.

The taster stood before the queen, looking down at the dish she now held in her hands. His eyebrows twitched, and the hairs on his arms stood on end as Katherine scooped up a small portion of the pudding from the top of the dish and fed it to the man. He chewed, keeping his eyes focused on Katherine with each slow chomp. She tightened her grip on the bowl she held, lessening the shaking of her hands.

The assayer narrowed his eyes. He glanced down at Katherine's hands, noting her white knuckles. Looking back to the queen, he subtly raised his eyebrows.

Katherine pursed her lips and stared back, holding a steady gaze.

Silence followed. The assayer's face relaxed. He rubbed his stomach, sent one last suspicious look to Katherine, and nodded. "This dish may be given to His Majesty," he said. Katherine's shoulders relaxed. The guard sent the assayer away, and Katherine was permitted entrance.

"Who has entered my chambers?" Henry asked when the door closed behind Katherine. He rolled his head to the side, but found he could not strain his neck enough to see. Katherine stifled a laugh at his struggle to lift his rotund body from the bed.

"Your queen, Katherine Parr," she said.

"Ah, Katherine, my love."

"It is glorious to see that your health has improved, My Lord."

"Yes, the doctor says it has soared." From the king's attempts to sit up, Katherine knew that the doctor had not dared to say otherwise to the monarch earlier in the day.

"As your health has improved, I brought you a surprise," Katherine said, placing the tray on a table behind the king's bed.

"How fitting," Henry responded.

Katherine looked about and saw that Henry's handmaids were

busy across the chamber, by his washroom. Knowing that the king could not see her from this position, she took out her bottle and unplugged the top. She paused, holding it with both hands. Frowning, she looked at the bottle, then glanced to the king's pudding. Three more drops were not nearly enough for what Katherine now intended. Four long years of waiting and working had passed. Katherine had reached the end. Half of the bottle's contents she poured on the pudding. The clear liquid blended in with the custard covering the dessert. The rest she poured into the mead in the tall goblet. The bottle that had spent years hidden within the folds of her dress was now empty, to the final drop. She plugged the bottle once again and dropped it back down her bodice. It was shockingly light against her chest. She took a deep breath before picking up the bowl and goblet. She rounded the bed to sit beside the king.

"What is it?" he asked, fat hands clawing at the bed sheets to push himself up. He managed to lift his head enough to look with squinted eyes at the pudding.

"Plum pudding," Katherine said.

"Oh, brilliant. Help me up, Katherine. Help me up."

Katherine placed the items down and reached up above the bed, tucking two wooden bars down and under Henry's arms. She pushed a lever down and the bars pulled Henry into a wilted sitting position. As he was pulled up, the king's sheets fell away, exposing his mangled leg and plump stomach. Years before their marriage, the king had fallen during a round of jousting, his old bones crackling under the impact. His destroyed leg made movement near impossible. As he could no longer ride or strut about the palace, his bountiful meals of mutton and salmon had caused the king to gain weight.

Katherine placed the pudding bowl on Henry's lap. She took a spoonful and held it to his lips. He opened his mouth, and she fed him the pudding. She bit her lip to quell her nervous anticipation while Henry chewed and swallowed.

After a few minutes of eating, Henry coughed and lifted a hand over his mouth. "Oh," he sputtered. "A drink, Katherine. Please." Katherine reached for the goblet by her side. She handed it to the king, and he tipped it back, draining half of the mead in seconds. He shuddered at the bitter taste, but soon his fit faded and his breathing steadied.

Katherine prepared another spoonful. "Are you all right, Majesty?"

"Indeed," the king said, puffing up his chest. "Perhaps I ought to eat in smaller portions. I am so full, and would dread overeating. My doctor would chide me if my stomach aches were to return."

"Of course." Katherine nodded. She looked at the goblet in Henry's hands. "I shall deal you smaller spoonfuls, my love. Please, drink and calm your breathing while I prepare."

Henry nodded and sipped from his cup. Katherine scraped her silver spoon along the top rim of the pudding, scooping up the soggiest layers. Wafting it past her nose to test the smell, she once again held the spoon up to her husband's mouth. He opened it and ate, bit by bit.

"Oh, my stomach cannot take any more." He groaned. "You have given me too much." He rubbed one large hand over his aching stomach.

"My apologies," Katherine said.

"I do not want your apologies, Katherine," Henry said, waving his hand at Katherine. "Take the remainder and leave."

Katherine looked down to the bowl. Half of the dish was left lying in a sopping mixture at the bottom. "Highness, are you certain you would not like another spoonful or two?" She pushed the runny pudding around the bowl with a spoon and then looked over to Henry.

"Katherine, be gone," Henry repeated. His hand lashed out and caught the edge of the queen's cheek. Katherine jolted backwards, almost dropping the bowl. She felt the mark of the king's fingers on her face. She glowered at the bitter king.

Pale-faced, he had leaned back hard onto his pillows. Ignoring his panting breaths, Katherine stood, placed the bowl on the tray, and began to leave. "Katherine..." Henry said, calling her back.

Katherine's lips curled into a tight smile. She turned to look at the king. "Yes, Majesty?"

He did not respond. Katherine looked at Henry's empty goblet. It teetered in his hand, threatening to fall from his weak grip. Henry squirmed and made a whimpering sound. She walked back to his side, took the goblet from his hand, and placed it beside the bowl.

"Katherine..." he mumbled. "Call for a doctor. The pain in my leg is burning. My entire body feels swollen with hurt."

Katherine paused, watching the man's chest move up and down with his short, wheezing breaths. "I shall," Katherine said. The queen waved a handmaid over and asked the girl to fetch a medical attendant for the king. She rushed outside the chambers. Katherine could hear her footsteps clatter down the stairs.

The queen turned back to Henry, who now lay with his mouth agape. He clutched his fingers against his stomach. Through winded breaths, he said, "What is this? Where does this pain arise from?" Katherine stayed silent. She walked to the king's bedside and sat down beside him. She placed her warm, clammy hand atop his fidgeting fingers. "Katherine?" He looked to her with wild eyes.

"My apologies, Henry." Her voice was flat as she looked down at the weakened ruler.

Henry narrowed his eyes.

"What have you to be sorry for?" the king demanded. Katherine looked down at the king's heaving chest, then returned her gaze to his glare.

"Katherine, what have you – " he began, but his need to gasp for air forced him to be silent. He attempted to shake her off, but found he was unable. Desperate attempts to get more air into his lungs made his face flush red. Black dots danced in front of his vision. Henry grabbed onto Katherine's arm, dirty fingernails pressing against her soft skin. "Katherine..." He grit his teeth together. "Why?"

Katherine shook her head. "You must understand," she said. She pulled her hands back. "This had to be done..." Katherine crossed her arms. "For Jane, for my namesake, for all those to come."

"Murder," Henry mustered, his voice scratchy and low. "Murder," he said again, barely audible. "Murder!" he whispered for the third time. Katherine walked over to the doors and lay her fists against their surface. Taking a deep breath, she began pounding on the doors.

"The king..." she shouted in false exasperation. "The king, he is dying."

The doors were ripped open, and the guard rushed to the king's side. Henry's mouth moved, but the only sound he managed was a weak, "M... m-m..."

"What does he say?" the guard asked, looking over his body in search of some way to assist the king.

Katherine tilted her head. "The monks..." she improvised. "He cries for the monks which he evicted from the monasteries. He calls for their forgiveness before his death," Katherine said. Guilt began to claw at her heart; the least she could do was make his last words noble ones. Cicely came up beside her and grasped her arm.

"Come, Lady Katherine. Let us away from this horrid scene. It will scar you so." Cicely removed her queen from the king's chambers and brought her to the great room, where the high walls of the castle towered around Katherine. She lowered herself to the floor by the fire, linking her fingers together. Cicely put a hand on Katherine's back, and the queen forced herself to softly cry. In a low voice, she repeated over and over, "My love, oh my love."

Cicely rubbed her back, looking down at her queen in sympathy. "The king shall rest peacefully in a high Heaven, My Lady."

"Indeed he shall," Katherine replied. The widowed queen smiled to herself, disguising her contented laughter as weeping for the killed king.

ACKNOWLEDGEMENTS

First and foremost, it seems only just to begin my acknowledgements by thanking my incredible editor, Charlotte Locklear, for her dedication and direction in the formation of this book. Without her, queens would be roaming gardens alone and sipping tea from green china cups. For all her help, I am immeasurably grateful.

From here, I would like to thank two constant enthusiasts: my parents. My mother, for her endless encouragement. My father, for his quiet support.

I must also thank my dearest friend, Alex. From freshman biology class to lounging together on beanbags, Alex has had my back. She has stuck with me through every high and low, and for that, I cannot be more thankful.

Thank you to Julia, as well, for taking the time to design a cover that so perfectly encapsulates my collection and brings to life each of my queens.

For Adolfo, I am especially grateful. His confidence in me and my work is unbelievable, and his support means nothing less than the world to me.

Finally, among the many others whom I would like to thank, I must convey my appreciation to my literary arts family, students and teachers alike. The entire group, from my classmates to Mrs. Supplee and Mrs. Tenly, has offered inspiration, support, and critique for this collection. It is because of all of these people that this book has landed in your hands.

ABOUT THE AUTHOR

Cerys Beckwith is a driven Literary Arts student, born in Wales and raised in Baltimore, Maryland. She is a senior at George Washington Carver Center for Arts and Technology, where she has been featured in both the school's literary magazine and newspaper. This collection is her first self-published book. Cerys hopes to continue pursuing writing in college while following a career path in International Affairs and Relations.